Bronson Howard

The Banker's Daughter

Lilian's Last Love - A Drama in Five Acts and Six Tableaux

Bronson Howard

The Banker's Daughter
Lilian's Last Love - A Drama in Five Acts and Six Tableaux

ISBN/EAN: 9783337118655

Printed in Europe, USA, Canada, Australia, Japan

Cover: Foto ©Andreas Hilbeck / pixelio.de

More available books at **www.hansebooks.com**

THE

BANKER'S DAUGHTER,

OR

LILIAN'S LAST LOVE.

A DRAMA

IN FIVE ACTS AND SIX TABLEAUX.

BY

BRONSON HOWARD.

PEOPLE IN THE PLAY.

-----oOo-----

JOHN STREBELOW.

HAROLD ROUTLEDGE.

COUNT DE CAROJAC.

LAWRENCE WESTBROOK.

DABBAGE.

G. W. PHIPPS.

MONTVILLAIS.

BROWN.

LILLIAN.

FLORENCE ST. VINCENT.

AUNT FANNY.

LIZETTE.

NATALIE.

FOOTMAN.

S C E N E.

S E T.

¦ HANDSOME LIBRARY IN THE HOUSE OF LAW-
RENCE WESTBROOK, NEW YORK. RICH FUR-
NITURE, INCLUDING HANDSOME JAPANESE
SCREEN.
AT RISE OF CURTAIN, ENTER R.U.D. WEST-
BROOK, FOLLOWED BY FOOTMAN. ¦

WEST.

¦ CROSSING AND SITTING L. OF TABLE. ¦ A POACHED EGG, SOME ANCHOVY
TOAST, A LITTLE CHETNA, SOME TEA; IN THE MEANTIME, THE PAPERS, AND
WHATEVER MAIL THERE IS. ¦ SITTING AT TABLE. ¦ I FEEL A SORT OF
SHIVERING SENSATION, I SEEM TO FEEL A DRAUGHT, PULL THAT SCREEN
AROUND HERE, THAT WILL DO; WHAT TIME IS IT?

FOOTMAN.

HALF PAST TWO, SIR. THE PAPERS ARE ON THE TABLE.

WEST.

VERY WELL! GET THE MAIL.

FOOTMAN.

YES, SIR. ¦ EXIT R.U.D. ¦

WEST.

¦ YAWNING AND SHIVERING, OPENING HERALD. ¦ I THINK BAGGAGE IS RIGHT
I MUST BE A FOOL, TO SIT UP LISTENING TO GOSSIP OF A SOCIETY I
REALLY TAKE NO INTEREST IN. WHAT THE DEUCE IS IT TO PLAIN LAW-
RENCE WESTBROOK, BANKER AND BROKER, WHO THE BEST SWORDSMAN IN PARIS
IS, THAT HE SHOULD SIT UP TILL FIVE IN THE MORNING TO HEAR IT DIS-
CUSSED? THAT CAROJAC MUST BE A WIZARD, THOUGH, IF HE PERFORMED
HALF THOSE FEATS. I SUPPOSE NOW, THAT FELLOW WOULD RATHER RUN A
MAN THROUGH THE BODY THAN INHERIT A FORTUNE. HE IS ABOUT THE ONLY

FOREIGN NOBLEMAN THAT NEVER ASKED ME TO CASH A NOTE FOR HIM.
{ ENTER FOOTMAN R. U. D. }
HE SAYS HE HAS A GREATER FAVOR THAN THAT TO ASK ME.

FOOTMAN.
{ NOW AT TABLE. }   THE MAIL, SIR.

WEST.
{ TAKING LETTERS OFF SALVER. }   VERY WELL.   { PLACES LETTERS ON
TABLE. }   SEE TO MY BREAKFAST.

FOOTMAN.
YES, SIR.   { EXIT R. U. D. }

WEST.
{ FIXING ON PARTICULAR COLUMN IN THE HERALD. }   MORE FAILURES!
LONDON CATCHES IT SOMETIMES AS WELL AS NEW YORK.   NONE OF THESE
CAN AFFECT US, HOWEVER.   THE GOLD BALANCE AT THE CLEARING HOUSE,
''TWO FOUR -- TWENTY - NINE, FIVE.''   HM!   HANG IT!   I CAN'T GET
UP ANY INTEREST IN ANYTHING.   { THROWS PAPER DOWN. }   LET ME SEE
THESE,   { OPENS LETTERS. }   BABBAGE OUGHT TO HAVE THIS.   { TAKES
UP ANOTHER. }   THE REGULAR QUARTERLY BILL OF LILLIAN'S DRESSMAKER.
{ TAKES UP ANOTHER. }   FROM STREDELOW!   WHAT CAN HE WRITE ABOUT?
I SAW HIM YESTERDAY.   { OPENS LETTER. }   READS. }   PERMISSION TO AD-
DRESS MY DAUGHTER AS A SUITOR.   { LOOKS PLEASED. }   THIS IS GRAT-
IFYING -- I KNOW FEW MEN I RESPECT MORE THAN JOHN STREDELOW.   I'M
SORRY!   IT WOULD NOT BE MAY AND DECEMBER, BUT IT WOULD BE MAY AND
OCTOBER.   STREDELOW MUST BE FORTY.   RICH, HONORED, WELL BORN, A
MAN OF UNUSUAL INTELLECT.   I WISH HE WERE BUT TEN YEARS YOUNGER,
{ LOOKS AT LETTER. }   WILL CALL FOR MY ANSWER THIS AFTERNOON.   HE
CAN HAVE MY PERMISSION, HE'LL NEVER GAIN HERS.

LILLIAN.
{ HEARD LAUGHING OUTSIDE. }   SERIOUS!   WHY, COUNT, I CAN'T BE SE-
RIOUS.

CAROJAC.
{ OUTSIDE.   SPEAKS WITH FRENCH ACCENT. }   WHEN WILL YOU BE?

LILLIAN.
{ BURSTING INTO ROOM, R.D.   RIDING HABIT; WHIP. }   WHENEVER YOU
ARE MERRY.

CAROJAC.

[FOLLOWING IN RIDING DRESS, WHIP.] BUT, MADEMOISELLE, YOU AL-
WAYS TREAT ME THE SAME WAY. YOU WILL NEVER GIVE ME THE ANSWER.
YOU PARRY ALL MY ATTACKS WITH A LAUGH.

LILLIAN.

[LAUGHINGLY.] WITH SO EXPERT A CHEVALIER I MUST FENCE AS BEST I
MAY. NO SHIELD SO SAFE AGAINST THE POINT OF A PROPOSAL AS A LADY'S
LAUGH, YOU KNOW -- THAT'S YOUR BALZAC'S ARHORISM. DO NOT LOOK SO
SAD. YOU SEEM LIKE A DON QUIXOTE HOLDING YOUR WHIP AS A SMALL
SWORD!

CARO.

[VEXED.] BUT --

LILL.

SOME OTHER DAY, COUNT, SOME OTHER DAY.

CARO.

I CANNOT WAIT; I MUST RETURN TO PARIS.

LILL.

[ARCHLY, CROSSING TO R.] GOOD-BYE! SEND ME SOME GLOVES.

CARO.

[BITTERLY.] . YOU WOULD NOT MOCK YOURSELF OF MR. ROUTLEDGE SO.

LILL.

SIR! YOU HAVE NO RIGHT!

CARO.

I OFFEND YOU -- I BEG YOUR PARDON. BUT I OFFER YOU --

LILL.

[ASIDE.] WHAT I DON'T WANT.

CARO.

THE HAND AND TITLE OF A GENTLEMAN, AND YOU WILL NOT GIVE ME AN AN-
SWER. BUT I WILL WAIT AND CALL TO-NIGHT.

LILL.

TO- MORROW.

CARO.

TO-NIGHT.

LILL.

INDEED! I SAY NOW NEXT WEEK -- NEXT MONTH -- NEXT YEAR, IF I WISH,
AND TILL THEN, COUNT DE CAROJAC, AU REVOIR.

: EXITS LAUGHING, SNAPPING HER WHIP, R.3.E:

CARO.

SHE MOCKS HERSELF OF ME. A WEEK AGO SHE WAS WITH ROUTLEDGE WHEN
I CALL, SHE MAKE SPORT OF ME THEN, TOO, AND HE LAUGH. IF I CATCH,
: CLUTCHING HIS WHIP : M. ROUTLEDGE IN PARIS, I MAY FIND A CHANCE
TO MAKE HIM SMILE WIZ DE ODER SIDE OF HIS MOUTH.

: GOING OFF R. I. E. :

WEST.

: FROM BEHIND SCREEN, LAUGHING. : COME HERE COUNT, COME HERE,
: WEST. RISES, COMES FORWARD. : YOU MUST NOT BE OFFENDED WITH
LILLIAN, SHE IS A SPOILED CHILD, BUT TO BE FRANK WITH YOU, I MUST
TELL YOU I AM PRETTY CERTAIN YOU HAVE NO CHANCE WITH HER. WITH
ALL HER GIDDINESS, IF SHE AT ALL ENTERTAINED YOUR PROPOSAL, SHE IS
NATURALLY TOO TRUE TO SO RECEIVE IT.

CARO.

THEN -- I WILL GO BACK TO PARIS. I ONLY WAIT HERE FOR HER ANSWER.
WHEN I HEAR HER ENGAGEMENT WITH M. ROUTLEDGE WAS, WHAT YOU CALL,
BROKE -- I FLATTER MEESELF I MIGHT -- : ENTER FANNY R.I.E.: AH,
MADAME HOLCOMB.

: BOWS.

FANNY.

: R : I HOPE, COUNT, YOU AND LILLIAN HAD A PLEASANT RIDE.

CARO.

: C : MLLE. WESTBROOK ENJOYED IT VERY MUCH. SHE LAUGHED ALL THE
TIME : ASIDE. : AT MY EXPENSE!

FANNY.

A BAD AUGURY FOR YOU, COUNT.

CARO.

OH, YES, I HAVE ~~HAD~~ MY CONJE', AND NOW WILL TAKE ME BACK TO PARIS.

M WESTBROOK, YOU WILL SOON, I HOPE, GIVE ME OPPORTUNITY TO REPAY
THERE, THE HOSPITALITY YOU TENDER ME HERE.

WEST.

[SHAKING HANDS WITH THE COUNT.]   I SHALL BE ONLY TOO HAPPY, COUNT,
BELIEVE ME.

CARO.

[CROSSING TO R.]   THEN GOOD-BYE.

WEST.

[L.C.]   A PLEASANT VOYAGE.

FANNY.

[C]   GOOD-BYE, COUNT.

CARO.

[TO WESTBROOK.]   MUCH THANKS.   [TO FANNY.]   GOOD-BYE.
[EXIT R. L. D.]

FANNY.

SO LILLIAN HAS REFUSED THE COUNT?

WEST.

[LAUGHING.]   SHE MERELY LAUGHED AT HIM.   I HAD TO DO THE REFUSING.

FANNY.

[SITTING ON OTTOMAN.]   WELL, I'M GLAD IT IS OVER.   SHE AND ROUT-
LEDGE FELL OUT ABOUT HIM; AND WHILE HE REMAINED HERE IT SEEMED
IMPOSSIBLE TO KNOW WHAT MIGHT HAPPEN.

WEST.

[LAUGHING.]   I CERTAINLY DID NOT WISH THE COUNT FOR A SON-IN-LAW,
AND I'M VERY GLAD MY LITTLE GIRL HAD TOO MUCH SENSE TO BE CAUGHT
BY HIS TITLE.   HIS CHARACTER IS NOT EXACTLY WHAT I LIKE, READY TO
QUARREL, A DUELLIST, AND SEEMING TO INHERIT BUT ONE INGREDIENT OF
HIS ANCESTORS' CHIVALRY, ITS COURAGE, AND BUT ONE QUALITY OF THEIR
WIT, ITS CYNICISM.   A CHARMING CLUB ACQUAINTANCE, BUT NO SON-IN-
LAW FOR ME.   BETTER HAROLD ROUTLEDGE, EVEN.

FANNY.

[APPROVINGLY.]   MUCH BETTER.

{ ENTER FOOTMAN R. U. E. }

FOOTMAN.

YOUR BREAKFAST IS READY, SIR.

WEST.

VERY WELL.

{ SERVANT PUTS SCREEN UP. }

FANNY.

{ RISING. }   YOUR BREAKFAST AT THREE IN THE AFTERNOON!

WEST. { CROSSING TO R. }

YES, I WAS UP LATE -- AT THE CLUB.   BUT I HAVE A BETTER HUSBAND
FOR LILLIAN THAN EITHER A FRENCH COUNT OR A POOR ARTIST.

FANNY.

A BETTER HUSBAND!   WHO?

WEST.

JOHN STREBELOW.

FANNY.

A NOBLE GENTLEMAN, BUT HE IS OLD -- TOO OLD FOR A WIFE OF EIGHTEEN.

WEST.

NOT FORTY YET.

FANNY.

BUT I'M SURE LILLIAN LOVES HAROLD ROUTLEDGE.

WEST.

PSHA!   I'LL BET SHE HAS FORGOTTEN HIM ALREADY.   BOYS AND GIRLS OF
EIGHTEEN HAVE WHIMS -- NOT LOVE.   YOU THOUGHT YOUR HEART WOULD
BREAK WHEN YOU MARRIED COMFORTABLE JOHN HOLCOMB INSTEAD OF ROMANTIC
ALFRED HARCOURT, YET YOU MADE A SPLENDID WIFE, AND A HAPPY ONE.

FANNY.

{ DRILY.   SITTING L. }   DID I?   YOU JUDGE BY WHAT YOU SEE, AND ALL
YOU SEE IS THE OUTSIDE.   WHERE A WOMAN IS CONCERNED THE BLINDEST
THING ON EARTH IS A MAN.

WEST.

WELL, WELL, SISTER, I'M NOT GOING TO SELL THE GIRL, WE'LL TALK OF
HER AGAIN, AFTER I'VE HAD MY BREAKFAST.

[EXITS R. U. D.]

FANNY.

[SOLUS.] SELL THE GIRL! NO -- NOT AT SO MUCH A POUND, I SUPPOSE!
BUT LIKE OTHER FATHERS YOU'LL SUPPLY HER A MENTOR WHERE SHE WANTS
A HUSBAND; AND GIVE HER A STONE WHERE SHE ASKS FOR BREAD, ON THE
PLEA THAT THE STONE IS A DIAMOND.

[SITS R. OF B. TABLE.]

[ENTER LILLIAN R. U. D.]

LILL.

[LAUGHING.] IS THE COUNT GONE? GOOD MORNING, AUNT.

[KISSED FANNY.]

FANNY.

YES, PET. SO YOU REFUSED HIM?

LILL.

OF COURSE I DID. COUNTSHIP, CASTLE, CHIVALRY AND ALL.   IT WAS SO
VERY FUNNY TO SEE HIM.

[LAUGHS.]

FANNY.

[LOOKING AT HER.]   I THOUGHT YOU WOULD.

LILL.

YOU KNEW   I WOULD. WHEN I LAUGHED AT HIM, WHICH WAS FROM THE
DOOR TO MT. ST. VINCENT, AND FROM MT. ST. VINCENT TO THE DOOR AGAIN,
HE LOOKED AS IF HE'D LIKE TO CALL ME OUT.

[LAUGHS.]

FANNY.

THIS IS THE FOURTH OFFER YOU HAVE REFUSED IN TWO WEEKS.

LILL.

IS IT? I DON'T WANT TO MARRY. I'M AS HAPPY AS A LARK AND JUST AS
GAY.   I'VE DONE NOTHING BUT LAUGH ALL THE MORNING.   IT WAS SUCH
FUN.

[LAUGHS HYSTERICALLY.]

FANNY.
[TAKING HER BY THE WAIST.]   LILLIAN, YOU ARE VERY MISERABLE.

LILL.
[LOOKS UP AT FANNY.   HER HYSTERICAL LAUGHTER GRADUALLY BECOMES
HYSTERICAL SOBBING, AND AS FANNY LEADS HER TO CHAIR L.H. SINKS INTO
IT AND BURSTS INTO TEARS.]   MY HEART IS BREAKING!

FANNY.
[SIGHING.]   I KNOW, DEAR -- I KNOW!   HAROLD ROUTLEDGE SAILS FOR
EUROPE TO-MORROW.

LILL.
[SOBBING.]   I'VE TRIED SO HARD -- SO HARD -- TO FORGET HIM.   I
SENT HIM BACK OUR EN -- ENGAGEMENT RING.   I'VE DONE ALL I COULD TO
DRIVE HIM FROM MY MIND.   I STAID UP?HALF THE NIGHT, READING ALL HIS
LETTERS BEFORE I -- I -- BURNED THEM.

FANNY.
MY POOR DARLING, LISTEN TO ME.   I LOST MY POOR ALFRED JUST IN THE
SAME WAY!   DON'T REPEAT MY MISTAKE.   WRITE TO HAROLD, TELL HIM TO
COME TO YOU.

LILL.
[RISING, CROSSING TO R.]   NEVER!   NEVER!   IF MY HEART WERE TO
BREAK A THOUSAND TIMES OVER I WOULD NOT DO THAT.   IT IS HIS PLACE
TO WRITE TO ME.   HE WAS IN THE WRONG.
                    [WALKS UP AND DOWN THE STAGE.]

FANNY.
IN THE WRONG?

LILL.
HE SHOULD HAVE KNOWN ME BETTER, THAN TO FLY AT ME ABOUT A MERE
FLIRTATION WITH THE COUNT DE CAROJAC.   HE KNEW WELL ENOUGH IT WAS
ALL IN FUN, MERE AMUSEMENT.

FANNY.
WELL, WELL, DEAR, LET ME WRITE TO HIM.   LET ME TELL HIM YOU HAVE
REFUSED THE COUNT.

                         LILL.
[DEMURELY.] BUT AUNT, HE MUST NOT THINK I ASKED YOU TO WRITE.

                              FANNY.
[SMILING.] CERTAINLY NOT.
                         [CROSSES TO R.]

                         LILL.
AND YOU'LL TELL HIM I REFUSED THREE OTHER OFFERS?

                              FANNY.
[SMILING.] INDEED I WILL.

                         LILL.
AND -- AND ASK HIM TO -- TO CALL AND SEE -- AND SEE YOU.

                              FANNY.
EXACTLY.

                         LILL.
[TAKING FANNY'S HEAD IN HER HANDS AND KISSING IT.] OH, YOU DAR-
LING GOOD AUNT!

                              FANNY.
[KISSING LILLIAN.] I AM DOING WHAT I KNOW YOUR MOTHER WOULD DO
IF SHE WERE ALIVE TO DO IT. WHAT [SIGHING] SHE WOULD HAVE DONE
FOR ME, HAD I BEEN WISE ENOUGH TO LET HER. I'LL GO TO MY ROOM AND
WRITE THE LETTER.

                         .LILL.
YOU'LL LET ME SEE IT?

                              FANNY.
CERTAINLY NOT. IT IS NONE OF YOUR BUSINESS, YOU KNOW.
                                                  [LAUGHS.]

                         LILL.
[WITH FRANK, HEARTY LAUGH THIS TIME.] AH, AH! OF COURSE NOT.
I FORGET, I'M SO HAPPY.

                              FANNY.
HEAVEN GRANT YOU MAY CONTINUE SO, MY DARLING.
                                        [EXIT R.U.E.]

LILL.

{ SOLUS. } WILL HE COME? { IN AFFECTED DOUBT. } I RATHER THINK
HE WILL. I WONDER HOW MY EYES LOOK. { GOES TO GLASS, LOOKS AT
HERSELF, TOUCHES UP HER HAIR. } I AM PRETTY SURE HE WILL COME.

{ ENTER FLORENCE ST. VINCENT. }

FLORENCE.

HOW DE DOO, LILLIAN?

LILL.

{ TURNING FROM GLASS. } FLORENCE!

FLORENCE.

{ SITTING ON SOFA. } RIDING WITH THE COUNT DE CAROJAC, EH? I SAW
YOU RIDE BY OUR HOUSE. ARE YOU TO BE A COUNTESS? ISN'T THE COUNT
MAGNIFICENT? THEY SAY HE'S FOUGHT SIX DUELS, AND HE'S A REAL GEN-
TLEMAN, FRESH FROM PARIS, LIKE THE NEW SPRING BONNETS JUST IMPORTED
I'VE BEEN ON THE BOULEVARD RIDING WITH GEORGE WASHINGTON PHIPPS,
BEHIND HIS NEW MATCHED TEAM, CHESTNUTS, 2.37 -- I SUPPOSE YOU'VE
HEARD THE NEWS?

LILL.

WHAT NEWS, DEAR?

FLORENCE.

I'M GOING TO BE MARRIED.

LILL.

{ ASTONISHED. } MARRIED? TO WHOM?

FLORENCE.

MUM! TO OLD MR. BROWN, THE MILLIONAIRE.

LILL.

TO MR. BROWN! WHY, HE IS NEARLY SEVENTY.

FLORENCE.

EXACTLY SIXTY-NINE THE TWENTY-EIGHTH OF LAST FEBRUARY. HE SAYS
HE'S ONLY FIFTY-NINE. BUT I KNOW BETTER. I WOULD NOT MARRY HIM
IF HE WERE ONLY FIFTY-NINE. FIFTY-TWO YEARS BETWEEN US, THERE
ALWAYS OUGHT TO BE SOME DIFFERENCE, YOU KNOW.

LILL.
SURELY, FLORENCE, YOU ARE NOT SERIOUS. YOUR FATHER CANNOT CONSENT
TO SUCH A SACRIFICE.

FLORENCE.
MY FATHER IS DELIGHTED! IT IS NOT EVERY MAN THAT HAS A SON-IN-LAW
OLD ENOUGH TO BE HIS FATHER-IN-LAW. MY YOUNGEST SON WILL BE
THIRTY-EIGHT YEARS OLD, WHEN THE MINISTER PRONOUNCES ME MR. BROWN'S
WIFE. I'LL BE A GRANDMOTHER. ONE OF MY GRAND-DAUGHTERS IS NEAR-
LY AS OLD AS I AM, ALREADY. BROWN IS A MILLIONAIRE, THREE TIMES
OVER AT LEAST. FATHER IS PRESIDENT OF A LIFE INSURANCE COMPANY,
AND HE KNOWS ABOUT SUCH THINGS. HE SAYS THE AVERAGE OF LIFE, OVER
SEVENTY, IS ABOUT FIVE YEARS. ALLOW FIVE MORE, FOR UNTOWARD ACCI-
DENT, TEN YEARS -- I'LL BE ONLY TWENTY-NINE. THAT'S YOUNG, YOU
KNOW, FOR A RICH WIDOW.

LILL.
OH, FLORENCE! MARRIAGE IS NOT A JOKE.

FLORENCE.
THEN I SHOULD LIKE TO KNOW WHAT IS. { LAUGHS. } I HAVEN'T BEEN
ABLE TO KEEP MY FACE STRAIGHT FIVE MINUTES AT A TIME, SINCE I TOLD
OLD MR. BROWN I'D BE HIS WIFE.
{ LAUGHS. }

{ ENTER FOOTMAN, FOLLOWED BY BABBAGE, R.U. }

FOOTMAN.
I'LL SPEAK TO MR. WESTBROOK, SIR.
{ EXIT R. U. D. }

LILL.
OH, MR. BABBAGE!
{ GOES TO HIM AS HE MOVES DOWN STAGE, AND
GIVES HIM BOTH HER HANDS. }

FLORENCE.
HOW DO YOU DO, MR. BABBAGE?

LILLIAN LOOK AT EACH OTHER AND LAUGH. :   I HAVE IMPORTANT BUSINESS
WITH YOUR FATHER, LILLIAN.
                              : MOVES TO MANTEL. LOOKS AT PAPERS. :

                              LILL.
: GOING. :   COME, FLORENCE.

                         FLORENCE.
: ASIDE TO LILL. AS THEY GO. :   BROWN IS, AT LEAST, FIFTEEN YEARS
OLDER THAN HE IS.
                    : LAUGHS. :

                         LILL.
FLORENCE!

                    : LILL AND FLORENCE EXIT. :

                         FLORENCE.
: BEYOND THE DOOR, LAUGHING. :   IT IS SUCH A JOKE ON BOTH OF US.
                    : HER LAUGH IS HEARD DYING AWAY IN THE
                      DISTANCE. :

                         BABBAGE.
: SITTING L.C. : FIFTY THOUSAND -- A HUNDRED AND FIFTY -- SIXTY-
FIVE -- THE REGISTERED BONDS -- THIRD NATIONAL.
                         : ENTER LEISURELY AND YAWNING, WESTBROOK. :

                         WESTBROOK.
AH, BABBAGE!

                         BABBAGE.
JUST UP?   THREE P.M.   EXCUSE MY DISTURBING YOU SO EARLY IN THE
MORNING.

                         WEST.
: SITTING ON OTTOMAN. :   RIGHT FROM THE OFFICE, I SUPPOSE.   FOR
HEAVEN'S SAKE, DON'T TALK BUSINESS TO ME TO-DAY, BABBAGE.   I WAS
OUT LATE LAST NIGHT, AND I HAVE A WRETCHED HEAD-ACHE.

                         BABBAGE.
SITTING L. C. :   YOU HAVE A HEAD-ACHE.   WELL, I'VE GOT SOMETHING
TO CURE YOUR HEAD-ACHE.

                         WEST.
EH?

BABBAGE.

WESTBROOK, YOU'RE A FOOL!

WEST.

THANK YOU.

BABBAGE.

HOW MUCH IS THIS HOUSE WORTH?

WEST.

SEVENTY-FIVE THOUSAND. WHY DO YOU ASK?

BABBAGE.

IS IT FREE FROM INCUMBRANCE.

WESTBROOK.

YE-ES. THAT IS -- NO. I PUT IT IN FOR A -- A COLLATERAL YESTERDAY,
A PRIVATE SPECULATION OF MY OWN, A MERE TEMPORARY MATTER.

BABBAGE.

HOW MUCH?

WEST.

FIFTY THOUSAND DOLLARS.

BABBAGE.

HAVE YOU HEARD THE NEWS?

WEST.

WHAT NEWS?

BABBAGE.

DO YOU WANT IT SUDDEN, OR DO YOU WANT IT GRADUAL? [PAUSE.] WEST
BROOK, THE FIRM OF BABBAGE AND WESTBROOK, BROAD STREET, WILL GO
INTO BANKRUPTCY AT THREE O'CLOCK, TO-MORROW AFTERNOON. [RISES.
WESTBROOK IS ABOUT TO START TO HIS FEET, BABBAGE HOLDS HIM DOWN
BY THE ARM AND RESUMES.] THE FIRM OF TRAPHAGEN AND TRAYNOR, LON-
DON, WENT INTO BANKRUPTCY THIS MORNING, NEWS BY CABLE, WE HOLD
THEIR PAPER FOR THREE HUNDRED AND SEVENTY-FIVE THOUSAND DOLLARS.
                              [WEST FALLS BACK STUPEFIED IN HIS CHAIR.]
HOW'S YOUR HEAD-ACHE?

WEST.
[RISING AND CROSSING TO R. C.] MY POOR DAUGHTER!

BABBAGE.
YOUR OWN DOINGS, WESTBROOK. THE LIFE OF A QUIET AND RESPECTABLE
BANKER DID NOT SATISFY YOU. YOU MUST PLAY THE ROTHSCHILD, THE
MERCHANT PRINCE, LIVE IN IMPERIAL STYLE, ENTERTAIN FOREIGN NOBLES,
MAKE YOUR DAUGHTER --

WEST.
DON'T, BABBAGE, DON'T.

BABBAGE.
WITH YOUR EXTRAVAGANCE AND YOUR PRIVATE SPECULATIONS, YOU'VE COM-
PELLED THE FIRM TO RUN TOO NEAR ITS CAPITAL, AND NOW --

WEST.
MY POOR DAUGHTER!

BABBAGE.
AND MINE! I HAVE THREE DAUGHTERS, FOUR SONS, AND DAMN IT! I'VE
GOT A WIFE. WOULD TO HEAVEN THAT WERE ALL! BUT OUR RUIN INVOLVES
OTHERS. YOU KNOW WHAT I MEAN, WESTBROOK. ''OUR DEPOSITORS.''
THE EARNINGS OF THE POOR -- OF THE LEGACY OF THE WIDOW, THE INHER-
ITANCE OF THE ORPHAN.

WEST.
MY GOD, IT IS TERRIBLE!
[RISING, CROSSES TO L. AND BACK TO L.C.]

BABBAGE.
WE NEED THIRTY THOUSAND TO FULLY MEET OUR PAPER TO-MORROW. I'VE
STRAINED EVERYTHING, EVERY BODY. WE CAN'T RAISE IT. IF THIS
HOUSE WERE ONLY FREE FROM INCUMBRANCE.

WEST.
IT IS NOT. IT IS HOPELESSLY INVOLVED.
[SITS AT L. H. TABLE.]

BABBAGE.
THEN RUIN MUST COME TO YOU AND YOURS, TO ME AND MINE, TO THOUSANDS
OF POOR, HONEST, HARD WORKING --

WEST.
{ RISING IN GREAT AGITATION. } THERE IS A WAY.

BABBAGE.
A WAY!

WEST.
{ TAKING STREBELOW'S LETTER. } HERE READ THIS -- I CAN'T.

BABBAGE.
{ AFTER PUTTING ON SPECTACLES, READS. } JOHN STREBELOW -- MISS
WESTBROOK'S HAND IN MARRIAGE! I SEE -- HAVING PAWNED YOUR HOUSE,
YOU WOULD PAWN YOUR CHILD. WESTBROOK, YOU'RE A FOOL!
{ RETURNS NOTE TO WEST. }

WESTBROOK.
BUT --

BABBAGE.
{ IN AGITATION. } DAMN ME! BUT I'D RATHER SEE THE FIRM OF BABBAGE
AND WESTBROOK GO TO THE DEVIL THAN SEE THE HAPPINESS OF THAT GIRL
SACRIFICED TO IT. BESIDES, YOUR DAUGHTER, LIKE YOUR HOUSE, IS
ENCUMBERED.

WEST.
WHAT DO YOU MEAN?

BABBAGE.
I MEAN THAT HAROLD ROUTLEDGE HOLDS A MORTGAGE ON THE PROPERTY.

WEST.
BUT LILLIAN AND MR. ROUTLEDGE HAVE HAD A SERIOUS DISAGREEMENT.
{ RINGS BELL. }

BABBAGE.
OF COURSE THEY HAVE. A WOMAN NEVER QUARRELS WITH A MAN SHE DOES
NOT LOVE; AND DAMN IT! NEVER TIRES QUARRELING WITH THE MAN SHE
DOES LOVE. YOU HAVE BEEN MARRIED, I AM MARRIED, WE BOTH KNOW IT.
{ ENTER FOOTMAN R. U. D. }

WEST.

YES, SIR.

: EXIT R. U. D. :

WEST.

I TAKE A DIFFERENT VIEW OF MY DAUGHTER'S HAPPINESS. I CAN HARDLY
HOPE TO AVERT THE TERRIBLE CALAMITY YOU ANNOUNCE, THROUGH THE WEALTH
OF MR. STREBELOW, THOUGH IT MAY POSSIBLY SO TURN OUT. I CERTAINLY
SHALL NOT ASK HIM FOR A CHECK, CONVERTIBLE TO-MORROW, IN EXCHANGE
FOR MY DAUGHTER'S HAND. BUT WITH JOHN STREBELOW HER FUTURE IS
SAFE, WHATEVER COMES TO US. TO GIVE HER TO SUCH A MAN IS NOT TO
SCARIFICE BUT TO SHIELD HER FROM THE STORM. THIS IS WHAT I WISH
TO DO. IF YOU CARE TO HEAR THE RESULT, I WILL JOIN YOU PRESENTLY
IN THE SITTING ROOM.

BABBAGE.

: GOING. : YES, I'LL WAIT. BUT IF THE CREDIT OF BABBAGE AND
WESTBROOK CANNOT BE SAVED WITHOUT THE SACRIFICE OF A YOUNG GIRL'S
HEART, I'D RATHER SEE IT CRUMBLE TO THE DUST, AND ACT AS ASSISTANT
BOOK-KEEPER TO A PEANUT STAND, FOR THE REST OF MY NATURAL LIFE.

: EXIT R. U. E. :

WEST.

: SOLUS. : IT IS NOT FOR MY SAKE, IT IS FOR HER OWN. NO GIRL
COULD BE THE WIFE OF A MAN LIKE STREBELOW AND NOT LEARN TO LOVE HIM.
SHE WILL BE PROVIDED FOR, SHE WILL KEEP HER RANK IN SOCIETY. WHAT
FATHER COULD DO OTHERWISE?

: ENTER LILLIAN, R.U.D. :

LILL.

IT QUITE TAKES MY BREATH AWAY.

WEST.

{ AT TABLE PRETENDING TO LOOK AT PAPERS. }   IT IS A GRAND OFFER.

LILL.

OF COURSE IT IS.

WEST.

AND YOU MAY WELL BE PROUD OF IT.

LILL.

INDEED I AM, PROUD, VERY PROUD.

WEST.

{ EAGERLY TURNING TO HER. }   THEN I MAY ANSWER, YES?

LILL.

OH, NO -- NO!

WEST.

NO -- WHY!

LILL.

I DO NOT LOVE MR. STREDFLOW, PAPA. I ESTEEM, REVERE HIM. BUT I --
I -- I NEVER THOUGHT OF HIM IN -- IN -- THAT WAY, YOU KNOW.

WEST.

YOU HAVE BROKEN OFF YOUR ENGAGEMENT WITH HAROLD BOUTLEDGE?

LILL.

{ AGITATED. }   YES, I -- I HAVE.

WEST.

YOU WOULD SOON LEARN TO LOVE MR. STREDFLOW. WHY, WHEN YOU WERE BUT
TWELVE YEARS OLD, YOU KNOW, YOU USED TO CALL HIM YOUR SWEETHEART;
YOUR OLD LIKING FOR HIM WILL SOON RETURN, AFTER YOU ARE MARRIED
TO HIM.

WEST.
[SITTING ON SOFA WITH LILL.]   LISTEN, MY CHILD.   I AM RUINED!
IN A FEW DAYS, I WILL HAVE NO HOME OF MY OWN, NO ROOF TO COVER YOU.

LILL.
[BEWILDERED.]   YOU, POOR!

WEST.
WORSE THAN POOR -- A BANKRUPT.   I WOULD SEE YOU SHELTERED FROM
WANTS, FROM HUMILIATIONS YOU HAVE NEVER YET KNOWN.

LILL.
I'M NOT AFRAID.   SO LONG AS I AM WITH YOU.
                                            [KNEELING.]

WEST.
[PUTTING HER ON SOFA.]   BRAVE GIRL!   BUT IT IS NOT ONLY POVERTY,
IT IS SHAME, DISGRACE. (IT IS NOT ONLY OURSELVES, IT IS HUNDREDS,
THOUSANDS, WILL FIND THEIR RUIN IN MINE!   WHO WILL HEAP UPON YOUR
FATHER'S HEAD THE CURSES OF THE POOR, THE WAIL OF THE WIDOW AND THE
TEARS OF THE ORPHAN. -- I CANNOT SURVIVE IT!
                        [RISING, GOING TO L. H.]

LILL.
[RISING.]   I SEE IT -- I SEE IT.   [WITH FORCED CALMNESS.]   AND
THIS MARRIAGE WOULD AVERT ALL THIS?

WEST.
[BACK TO L.C.]   IT WOULD SAVE US ALL.   THANK GOD!   YOUR MOTHER
WAS SPARED THIS MISERY.

LILL.
MOTHER!   FATHER -- I -- I WILL -- I --

WEST.
MAKE THIS SACRIFICE -- I MEAN -- GIVE YOUR HAND?

LILL.
MY MOTHER'S LAST WORDS TO ME WERE, ''DO ALL YOU CAN TO MAKE YOUR
FATHER'S OLD AGE HAPPY.''

WEST.
[AVERTING HIS HEAD.]   ONE WORD WILL SAVE IT FROM INFAMY.

LILL.

THEN I SAY IT -- YES! : EMBRACE. : BUT BEFORE YOU REPEAT THAT
WORD TO MR. STREBELOW, YOU MUST PROMISE ME ONE THING.

WEST.

ANYTHING.

LILL.

IT IS THIS. YOU WILL TELL MR. STREBELOW THAT I WILL -- BE -- HIS--
WIFE! : PAUSE. : THAT I WILL ACCEPT HIM, IF HE WILL ACCEPT MY
HAND WITHOUT -- WITHOUT THE HEART I CANNOT NOW GIVE HIM; AND BE
SATISFIED WITH GRATITUDE AND RESPECT, INSTEAD OF LOVE!
: CROSSES TO L. H. :

: ENTER FOOTMAN, GIVES CARD TO WESTBROOK. :

WEST.

MR. STREBELOW. CERTAINLY, CERTAINLY, SHOW HIM IN.

: FOOTMAN ABOUT TO EXIT. :

LILL.

: TO FOOTMAN. : STOP -- ONE MOMENT -- YOU : TO WEST. : WILL DO
WHAT I ASKED?

WEST.

YES.

LILL.

: TO FOOTMAN. : YOU CAN GO. : EXIT FOOTMAN R. D. : I COULD NOT
TRUST MYSELF TO MAKE SUCH AN EXPLANATION TO MR. STREBELOW. I WILL
LEAVE YOU WITH HIM, FATHER, AND TAKE WITH ME YOUR PROMISE TO BE AS
FRANK WITH HIM AS I HAVE BEEN WITH YOU. THEN IF HE WILL HE CAN
TAKE ALL I HAVE LEFT TO GIVE -- MY HAND.
: STAGGERS. :

WEST.

BUT SIT DOWN, THE SUDDENNESS OF THIS HAS MADE YOU FAINT.

LILL.

ONLY A LITTLE. I -- I DON'T THINK I WILL SIT DOWN. I MIGHT LACK
THE STRENGTH TO RISE AGAIN.

FOOTMAN.

[ANNOUNCING.]   MR. STREBELOW.

[ENTER STREBELOW.]

WEST.

[GOING TO MEET HIM, THEY SHAKE HANDS.]   MY DEAR STREBELOW, I'M
DELIGHTED TO SEE YOU, AND TO SEE YOU LOOKING SO? WELL.

STREB.

THANKS.   [CROSSING TO LILL; BOWING.]   MISS WESTBROOK,   [HOLDS
OUT HIS HAND;   SHE PLACES HERS IN IT, CLINGING TO THE CHAIR AS IF
FOR SUPPORT.]   MAY I HOPE MY VISIT IS EQUALLY WELCOME TO YOU?

LILL.

[WITH FORCED CALMNESS.]   SO OLD A FRIEND CANNOT BE OTHERWISE THAN
WELCOME.

STREB.

I WAS IN HOPES YOUR FATHER HAD PLACED ME BEFORE YOU IN A MORE --
I MEAN IN A DIFFERENT LIGHT THAN THAT OF A MERE FRIEND.

LILL.

MY FATHER HAS HANDED ME YOUR NOTE, MR. STREBELOW --

[STOPS SHORT.]

STREB.

NOT, I TRUST, WITHOUT THE ENDORSEMENT OF HIS APPROVAL.

[LOOKS AT WEST.]

WEST.

I BELIEVE LILLIAN CAN BEST TELL YOU HOW MUCH I APPROVE OF IT.]

STREB.

[TO LILL.]   LET HIM HOPE THAT TO YOUR FATHER'S APPROVAL, YOUR
OWN IS ADDED.   AND THAT -- [SEEMS EMBARRASSED BY LILLIAN'S AT-
TITUDE.] AND THAT I MAY -- EXPECT AN ANSWER.

[TAKES HER HAND.]

LILL.

[GIVING HAND MECHANICALLY.]   I -- I MUST REFER YOU TO HIMSELF.

STREB.

AND AFTER I HAVE SEEN HIM, MAY I NOT SEE YOU?

LILL.

[FEEBLY.] CERTAINLY. FATHER!

WEST.

[CROSSING TO LILLIAN, SHE TAKES HIS ARM AND WALKS TO THE DOOR.
TURNS, BOWS TO STREBELOW.] YOU WILL EXCUSE LILLIAN AND MYSELF A
MOMENT.

[EXIT WEST, SUPPORTING LILL. R.U.D.]

STREB.

[SOLUS. CROSSING TO L.] IS MY SUIT ACCEPTED UNDER PROTEST, OR
IS THE STRANGENESS OF HER MANNER THE EFFECT OF MERE TIMIDITY -- A
TIMIDITY PROBABLY INCREASED BY MY FORMALITY? STILL -- THERE WAS
AN EXPRESSION OF SUPPRESSED EMOTION. THAT MAY BE EITHER FLATTER-
ING OR FATAL TO MY AFFECTION. THOSE RUMORS TOO, THAT I HAVE HEARD
ON THE STREET. I WILL KNOW THE TRUTH FROM WESTBROOK -- I MUST --
IN JUSTICE TO HER -- IN JUSTICE TO MYSELF.

[ENTER WESTBROOK, R. U. D.]

WEST.

[GOES TO STREBELOW WITH OUTSTRETCHED HANDS.] JOHN, I CONGRATU-
LATE YOU.

STREB.

THEN I AM ACCEPTED.

WEST.

WHY, CERTAINLY. SIT DOWN.

STREB.

[ON SOFA C.] WESTBROOK, AT SUCH A MOMENT, FRANKNESS IS A DUTY,
AND YOU WILL EXCUSE IT IN A MAN TO WHOM YOU ENTRUST YOUR DAUGHTER'S
HAPPINESS, AND WHO TRUSTS HIS OWN TO HER.

WEST.

[EMBARRASSED.] CERTAINLY, CERTAINLY.

STREB.

MY PROPOSAL, THOUGH LONG CONTEMPLATED BY MYSELF MUST HAVE APPEARED
SUDDEN TO YOU, STILL MORE SUDDEN TO YOUR DAUGHTER. PERMISSION TO
ADDRESS HER AS A SUITOR WAS ALL I EXPECTED. HER TIMID MANNER,
AND HER --

WEST.
[TRYING TO MAKE LIGHT OF IT.]   TUT, TUT! A GIRL OF EIGHTEEN.
BESIDES SHE HAS BEEN RIDING ALL THE MORNING, HER NERVES ARE OUT OF
ORDER, AND SHE IS TIRED.

STREB.
[WATCHING HIM.]   AND SHE IS YIELDING TO NO INFLUENCE OF YOUR'S?

WEST.
[EMBARRASSED.]   WHY SHOULD YOU THINK SO?

STREB.
FRANKLY THEN, BECAUSE I HAVE HEARD TO-DAY, THAT THE FIRM OF BADBAGE
AND WESTBROOK IS LIKELY TO GO TO PROTECT TO-MORROW.

WEST.
MR. STREBELOW!
                          [RISING.]

STREB.
IS IT TRUE?

WEST.
[HESITATINGLY.]   WE -- WE ARE -- A LITTLE DRIVEN FOR READY MONEY.

STREB.
HOW MUCH WILL BE NECESSARY TO MAKE YOUR PAPER GOOD?

WEST.
ONLY THIRTY THOUSAND DOLLARS.

STREB.
[RISING.]   MAY I WRITE HERE?
                          [SITTING AT TABLE L.]

WEST.
[FEIGNING ASTONISHMENT.]   WHY NOT?

STREB.
THIS IS THE 17TH --

STREB.

I WILL MEET YOUR DEFICIENCIES, MR. WESTBROOK.

WEST.

WHAT, YOU?

STREB.

YOU CAN GIVE ME WHAT SECURITY YOU PLEASE, AND AT YOUR OWN CONVEN-
IENCE.   HERE IS A CHECK FOR THE AMOUNT YOU REQUIRE.   DID YOUR
DAUGHTER KNOW OF YOUR FINANCIAL TROUBLES?

WEST.

: WITH EFFORT. :   SHE DID NOT.

STREB.

THEN I WRONGED YOU BOTH, CALM AND FORMAL AS I AM, I HAVE LONG LOVED
YOUR DAUGHTER.   I WAS HER KNIGHT, HER CHAMPION IN THOSE OLD DAYS,
SHE USED TO SAY I WOULD BE HER SWEETHEART; SHE WOULD LAY HER HEAD
UPON MY HEART AND GO TO SLEEP THERE.   THE LITTLE THING SEEMED TO
NESTLE INTO IT; AND I BELIEVE SHE HAS NEVER FAIRLY GROWN OUT OF
IT.   HER HAPPINESS IS MY FIRST CONSIDERATION, AND I -- AND I DID
NOT WISH -- BUT YOU ARE FREE NOW, AND YOUR FREE ANSWER IS --

WEST.

YES.

STREB.

: SHAKING HANDS WITH WEST. :   PARDON MY FRANKNESS, AND ACCEPT MY
THANKS.   MAY I SEE HER?

WEST.

: RINGING BELL. :   OF COURSE.
                    : CROSSING TO L. :

STREB.

IT WILL BE THE ENDEAVOUR OF MY LIFE TO RENDER HER HAPPY.   A SOLI-
TARY MAN, SHE WILL HAVE ALL MY CARE, ALL MY LOVE, AND IF HER FATHER
NEEDS MY AID, HE HAS ONLY TO SPEAK.

: ENTER FOOTMAN, R. U. D. :

WEST.

TELL MISS LILLIAN, MR. STREDELOW IS WAITING FOR HER. [EXIT FOOT-
MAN.] TO STREB.] THERE IS NOT A MAN IN THE WORLD TO WHOM I WOULD
SO CONFIDENTLY TRUST HER, AND I KNOW THAT IN GIVING HER TO YOU I
DO ALL A FATHER CAN DO TO INSURE HER HAPPINESS, AND IT IS IN THAT
BELIEF I DO WHAT I AM DOING.

LILL.

[ENTER R.U.D.] MR. STREDELOW!

STREB.

LILLIAN! I MAY CALL YOU THAT NOW?

LILL.

MY FATHER HAS TOLD YOU.

STRED.

YOUR FATHER HAS TOLD ME ALL.

[HOLDS OUT HIS HAND.]

LILL.

SO BE IT, THEN.

[GIVES HIM HER HAND, SHE KISSES IT.]

FANNY.

[ENTERING R.U.D.] MR. STREDELOW!

STRED.

[BOWS.] MRS. HOLCOMB!

FANNY.

WILL YOU EXCUSE ME, I HAVE A WORD TO SAY TO LILLIAN.

WEST.

MR. STEBELOW, IF YOU WILL ACCOMPANY ME TO THE SITTING ROOM, BAGGAGE
AND I WILL EXPLAIN TO YOU HOW THIS SUDDEN STRAI HAS ARISEN, OWING
TO THE FAILURE OF A FIRM IN LONDON WHOSE PAPER WE LARGELY HOLD.

[EXITS R.I.E.]

                              LILL.
HAROLD!

                              FANNY.
YES.   HE'S IN THE RECEPTION ROOM.   HE KISSED ME FOR JOY.

                              LILL.
{ WRINGING HER HANDS. }   OH, WHAT HAVE I DONE! WHAT HAVE I DONE!
                                   { CROSSES TO R. }

                              FANNY.
I TOLD HIM I WOULD SEND YOU TO HIM.   HE CANNOT SIT STILL A MOMENT,
NOT ONE MOMENT.

                              LILL.
SEE HIM -- I WILL -- I WILL.   { AT DOOR, RINGS BELL. }   BUT NOW,
HEAVENS! I DARE NOT.   { ENTER FOOTMAN. }   TELL MR. ROUTLEDGE --
THAT MISS WESTBROOK CANNOT -- CANNOT SEE HIM.   { GOES TO FANNY. }
I HAVE CONCLUDED NOT TO SEE -- NEVER AGAIN TO SEE -- HAROLD -- MR.
ROUTLEDGE!

                              FANNY.
{ SURPRISED. }   WHY?

                              LILL.
BECAUSE --   { STEADIES HERSELF. }   AUNT FANNY -- MR. STREBELOW IS
TO BE MY HUSBAND!   MY HEART IS BROKEN.
                    { FALLS ON OTTOMAN. }

                    C U R T A I N.

A C T   2.

---:0:---

S E T.

GRAND MODERN SALON IN THE PARISIAN RESI-
DENCE OF JOHN STREDELOW.

TIME-- MIDWINTER.

PEOPLE IN THE ACT. STREDELOW, OPEN
ROUTLEDGE-- CAROJAC, WESTBROOK, MONTVIL-
LAIS, BROWNE, LILLIAN NOW MRS. STREDELOW,
FLORENCE ST. VINCENT NOW MRS. BROWN,
NATALIE CHILD OF SIX.

THE CURTAIN RISES ON LILLIAN AND NATALIE.
THE FORMER IS SEATED AT PIANO THE LATTER
STANDING BY HER SIDE. L., AT PIANO.

NAT.

OH-- NO-- NO! I WANT YOU TO SING SOME MORE.

LILL.

BUT THERE IS NO MORE, DEAR.

NAT.

[IMPERVIOUSLY] THEN MAKE SOME MORE.

LILL.

MY DEAR, I AM NOT ABLE TO DO THAT.

NAT.

[KISSING HER.] NOW SING HOW MUCH YOU LOVE ME.

LILL.

I AM AFRAID EVEN THOMAS MOORE CANNOT HELP ME TELL YOU THAT DEAR.

NAT.

OH SEE IN THE BOOK. [DRAWS LILLIAN OVER TO R. TAKES VOL. OF IRISH
MELODIES OFF TABLE R. H. AND HOLDS IT UP TO
HER OPENING IT HAP-HAZARD.]

LILL.

[TAKING BOOK.] THIS, THIS TELLS THE STORY.

NAT.

OH DO SING.

LILL.

[SINGS] I'D MOURN THE HOPES THAT LEAVE ME, IF THY SMILE HAD
LEFT ME TOO
"MOORE'S IRISH MELODIES."
[CATCHING NATALIE IN HER ARMS AND LIFTS HER TO HER LAP.] SO IT
DOES, DARLING! SO IT DOES! [KISSES HER.]

        [WEST. HAS ENTERED R.C. AT THE LAST LINE
        OF THE LAST VERSE; AND STOPS AT THRES-
        HOLD LOOKING AT THEM.]

        WEST.

THANK HEAVEN! I WISH FANNY HOLCOMB COULD SEE THIS FALSIFICATION
OF HER PROPHESIES, THIS JUSTIFICATION OF MY WISDOM.

NAT.

[SEES HIM OVER HER MOTHER'S SHOULDER.] OH, MAMA, A GENTLEMAN--
IS THIS GRANDPAPA?

WEST.

[COMING DOWN STAGE AS LILL. PUTS NAT. DOWN] YES-- GRANDPAPA COME
AT LAST!
        [OPENS HIS ARMS TO HER-- NAT. RUSHES
        INTO THEM KISSES HER.]

LILL.

OH, FATHER.
        [THEY EMBRACE.]

        WEST.

NATALIE HAD ALMOST FORGOTTEN ME, EH?

NAT.

YOUR HAIR HAS GROWN SO WHITE.

3

WEST.

{PATTING NAT'S HEAD.} IT IS A LONG TIME SINCE IT LOOKED LIKE YOURS
{TO LILL.} BUT YOU SEEM SURPRISED TO SEE ME. DID YOU NOT RE-
CEIVE MY TELEGRAM? {PUTTING NAT, DOWN.}

LILL.

NO. NOTHING BUT YOUR LETTER ANNOUNCING YOUR INTENDED DEPARTURE
BY THE EUROPA.

WEST.

I WROTE YOU FROM LIVERPOOL-- AND TELEGRAPHED YOU FROM DOVER. BUT
HOW IS JOHN.

> {ENTER STREB. R. 3. E. WITH LETTER AND
> TELEGRAM IN HAND.}

STREB.

{AS HE ENTERS.} A LETTER FROM YOUR FATHER, LILLIAN DATED LIVER-
POOL. HE OUGHT TO BE HERE.

WEST.

HE IS HERE.

> {STREB. CROSSES TO HIM.}

STREB.

{SHAKING HANDS.} SO YOU HAVE COME AT LAST-- AFTER THESE YEARS
PROMISING.

WEST,

BUSINESS WAS SUCH I COULD NOT GET AWAY.

STREB.

AND PROSPERITY HAS WAITED ON ATTENTION?

WEST,

YES. THANK HEAVEN WE HAVE STEERED OVER ALL THE BREAKERS AND STAND
ON A FIRM SHORE AT LAST.

STREB.

AND CARRAGE?

WEST.

{SMILING.} JUST AS HAPPY AND JUST AS SURLY AS HE CAN BE.

4

STREB.

{LAUGHS.} BUT WHAT DO YOU THINK OF NATALIE AND LILLIAN?

WEST.

AS I LOOK AT BOTH I THINK JOHN STREBELOW MUST BE THE HAPPIEST
MAN ON EARTH.

LILL.

OH, FATHER! {TAKING NATALIE} BUT I MUST GO DRESS THE CHILD--   I
SUPPOSE YOU AND MR. STREBELOW HAVE A GOOD DEAL TO SAY TO EACH
OTHER-- SO I'LL LEAVE YOU FOR A WHILE--   COME DEAR.

NAT.

BUT I CAN COME AND SEE GRANDPAPA AGAIN AFTER I'M DRESSED.

LILL.

CERTAINLY.

STREB.

{TO LILL.} WHY NOT LET LISETTE DRESS HER DEAR?

LILL.

{HESITATING.} YES-- BUT . . . .

NAT.

NO-- NO. MAMA PROMISED TO DRESS ME HERSELF TO SEE GRANDPAPA--
COME-- MAMA, COME-- SO I CAN COME BACK SOON!
{PULLS LILL. OUT R. I. E.}

LILL.

{TURNING AT DOOR.} IS SHE NOT LOVELY?
{EXITS.}

WEST.

{VISIBLY AFFECTED.} _I SHOULD LIKE TO THANK YOU FOR THE HAPPINESS
YOU HAVE CONFERRED ON ME AND MINE ....BUT,....I,...I CAN'T MY SON...
I CAN'T.

STREB.

{R.} I'VE DONE MY BEST TO MAKE HER HAPPY . . . I BELIEVE SHE IS
SO-- THOUGH AT TIMES, I CANNOT HELP NOTICING A SADNESS OF LOOK AND
TONE THAT SELDOM LEAVES HER SAVE WHEN WITH HER CHILD.

5

WEST.
THEY WERE BOTH GAY ENOUGH WHEN I CAME IN-- LAUGHING-- SINGING--
KISSING.

STREB.
{THOUGHTFULLY.} HER WHOLE HEART IS WRAPT UP IN HER CHILD. . . .
IF I WERE A YOUNGER HUSBAND I MIGHT BE JEALOUS OF THE ABSORBING
LOVE SHE BEARS IT.

WEST.
{LAUGHING} THE LAW OF NATURE! THE HUSBAND IS NUMBER ONE TILL
BABY COMES-- THEN HE BECOMES NUMBER TWO! AND, AFTER ALL, A HUS-
BAND MAY WELL CONTENT HIMSELF WITH THE SECOND PLACE IN HIS WIFE'S
HEART WHEN HE KNOWS 'TIS ONLY A MINIATURE OF HIMSELF THAT FILLS
THE FIRST. {GIVES HIM BUNDLE OF N. Y. PAPERS.}

LISETTE.
{ANNOUNCING.} M. AND MAD. DE BROWNE. {AFTER FLORENCE, LISETTE
REMAINS STANDING AT DOOR. FLORENCE DROPS COURTESY TO STREB.}

FLORENCE.
{DOWN C.} HOW IS THE DUKE DE STREBELOW THIS MORNING-- WHERE IS THE
DUCHESS? IS LILLIAN WELL-- AH-- THE MARQUIS DE WESTBROOK--SO--
YOU HAVE ARRIVED AT LAST-- HOW DE DOO-- HOW IS EVERYBODY IN NEW
YORK?

WEST.
{SHAKING HANDS.} DELIGHTED TO SEE YOU.

STREB.
{LAUGHING} MY DEAR MRS. BROWN YOU LAVISH YOUR TITLES WITH SUCH
PRINCELY GENEROSITY, THAT WE POOR REPUBLICANS . . . .

FLOR.
''WE REPUBLICANS! '' HOW I HATE THAT WORD! AMERICANS IN PARIS
ARE AT SUCH A DISADVANTAGE IN SOCIETY. I AM PRESENTED TO MADAME
LA COUNTESSE DE POMPADILLICONA-- LACABELLA DE PONTVILLE, FOR IN-
STANCE-- AS PLAIN MRS. BROWNE, MRS. B. R. O. W. N. E. I HAD TO
ADD THE E MYSELF, BROWNE IS NEARLY SEVENTY-SIX YEARS OLD, YOU KNOW.
PERHAPS I'LL MARRY A DUKE SOME DAY-- OR A RUSSIAN PRINCE-- OR AN
ITALIAN NOBLEMAN, FRESH-- FROM THE ALMS HOUSE.

STREB.

{HUMORING HER.} HOW IS HIS HIGHNESS-- YOUR ROYAL CONSORT-- THE
PRINCE DE BROWNE, THIS MORNING?

FLOR.

THE PRINCE DE BROWNE IS IN HIS USUAL HEALTH-- THAT IS-- HE HAS
THE GOUT. HE IS COMING UP STAIRS NOW. BROWN HAS THE GOUT IN ITS
MOST ARISTOCRATIC FORM. IF HE WERE A LINEAL DESCENDANT OF WIL-
LIAM THE CONQUEROR'S ENTIRE ARMY, HE COULDN'T HAVE IT WORSE
{WALKS TO DOOR AND LOOKING OUT} HERE COMES THE PRINCE HIMSELF.
                    {ENTER BROWN C. EXTREMELY SENILE--HOBBLES
                    ON A CANE ONE LEG BOUND UP IN BANDAGES_. .
                    HE IS RICHLY DRESSED. FLORENCE PATS HIM.}

BROWN.

HE--HE-- EH-- HE! MY DEAR! {PATTING FLORENCE UNDER CHIN, KISSES
HER.} YOU GOT UP STAIRS BEFORE ME-- DIDN'T YOU? . . . STREBELOW,
MY DEAR FELLOW! MR. WESTBROOK {CROSSES TO HIM} GOT IN AT LAST,
EH, WELL? {SHAKES HANDS WITH WESTBROOK.}

WEST.

VERY WELL, THANKS-- BUT I'M SORRY TO SEE YOU SO LAME.

BROWN.

ONLY A TEMPORARY ATTACK, MY DEAR BOY. I'LL BE OVER IT IN SIX
WEEKS. WHEN SUCH A THING ATTACKS VERY OLD MEN, THEY LACK VITALITY
TO THROW IT OFF. {TO STREBELOW.} BUT WITH A MAN OF YOUR AGE OR
MINE, YOU KNOW-- {STREB. TURNS TO HIDE A LAUGH-- AS FLORENCE
NUDGES WESTBROOK.} THE ENERGY AND ELASTICITY OF NATURE SOON OVER-
COME ITS FORCE. THESE PREMATURE ATTACKS MAKE SOME PEOPLE THINK
I'M OLD. IT MAKES IT APPEAR AS IF THERE WERE SOME INAPPROPRIATE
DIFFERENCE-- SO TO SPEAK-- BETWEEN MY WIFE'S AGE AND MY OWN.
{PATS FLORENCE UNDER CHIN.} WE KNOW BETTER-- DON'T WE, MY LOVE?
THERE ISN'T A BETTER MATCHED COUPLE IN THE WORLD. HE . . . . HE!
BUT TIME WILL FLY, I SUPPOSE. HEIGHHO! FLORENCE AND I WILL SOON
BE GROWING OLD TOGETHER.

FLOR.

BROWNE, MY DEAR, YOU HAVEN'T HAD YOUR AFTERNOON NAP YET. {UP TO
DOOR.}

7

BROWNE.

HE-- HE-- HE-- YES-- YES! DURING THESE TEMPORARY ATTACKS I DO
LIKE AN AFTERNOON NAP-- NOW AND THEN-- I'LL GO INTO THE SMOKING
ROOM-- AND DROP DOWN ON THE LOUNGE, I SAY, WESTBROOK, COME WITH ME
AND TELL ME THE NEWS FROM NEW YORK AND PUT ME TO SLEEP. {MOVES L.}
WE REGARD THIS AS LIBERTY HALL-- WESTBROOK-- STREBELOW LIKES IT.
{STREBELOW ASSENTS IN DUMB SHOW} REALLY I AM GETTING AS MUCH AT-
TACHED TO THESE AFTERNOON NAPS AS IF I WERE A DECREPID OLD MAN.
IF I DON'T GET WELL SOON I DARE SAY THE HABIT WILL BECOME SO CON-
FIRMED I'LL KEEP UP MY NAPS FOR THE NEXT FIFTY YEARS.

> {HOBBLES OUT L. 3. E. FOLLOWED BY WEST-
> BROOK.}

FLORENCE.

{IN ALARM.} FIFTY YEARS. ! STREBELOW, I'M REALLY ANXIOUS ABOUT
THE PRINCE.

STREB.

NO NEED TO BE ANXIOUS, MY DEAR MRS. BROWN-- I DARE SAY HE'LL LAST
FOR TWENTY YEARS YET. HE COMES OF A LONG AND LINGERING FAMILY.

FLORENCE.

{WITH WRY FACE.} THAT'S COMFORTING. {GOES TO EASEL.} BUT HOW DO
YOU LIKE LILLIAN'S PORTRAIT NOW IT IS FINALLY FINISHED?

STREB.

THE EXPRESSION IS, I THINK, TOO SAD.

FLOR.

YOU CANNOT BLAME THE ARTIST FOR THAT. I HAVE NOT HEARD A HEARTY
LAUGH FROM LILLIAN--SINCE SHE HAS BEEN MARRIED.

STREB.

THAT'S VERY COMFORTING.

FLOR.

ONLY TIT FOR TAT. YOU HAVE INVITED M. MONTVILLAIS THE ARTIST AND
M. DE CAROJAC TO SEE THE PICTURE THIS AFTERNOON.

8

STREB.
YES, BEFORE IT DISAPPEARS FROM PROFANE EYES FOREVER IN LILLIAN'S
BOUDOIR--

FLOR.
BY THE WAY I SUPPOSE YOU KNOW THE COUNT DE CAROJAC HAS BEEN MAKING
DESPERATE LOVE TO YOUR WIFE LATELY.

STREB.
HAS HE?

FLOR.
HAS HE? IS THAT ALL YOU HAVE TO SAY ABOUT IT? I EXPECTED . . .

STREB.
¡LAUGHING.¡ WHAT?

FLOR.
THAT YOU WOULD FLY INTO A PASSION . . . TEAR YOUR HAIR . . . SEC-
ONDS . . . PISTOLS . . .

STREB.
¡LAUGHING¡ I HAVE NO DESIRE TO FACE THE MOST DANGEROUS DUELIST IN
PARIS. BESIDES DE CAROJAC IS A FRIEND OF MINE, AND AS A FRENCH
GENTLEMAN, CONSIDERS IT HIS DUTY TO PROVE HIS FRIENDSHIP BY MAKING
LOVE TO MY WIFE-- IN COMPLIMENT TO MY TASTE.

FLOR.
AND WHAT DO YOU CONSIDER YOUR DUTY AS AN AMERICAN HUSBAND?

STREB.
¡SERIOUSLY.¡ YOU FORGET I HAVE AN AMERICAN WIFE.

FLOR.
I WONDER IF BROWNE HAS THE SAME CONFIDENCE IN MY NATIONALITY.

STREB.
¡LAUGHING AND GOING TOWARD DOOR L.¡ I WILL INFORM THE DUCHESS DE
STREBELOW THAT YOU ARE HERE, SPEAKING OF FEMALE NATIONALITY IN
CONNECTION WITH THE DUTIES OF A WIFE, I FIND IT VERY HARD TO REALIZE
THAT MRS. BROWNE . . . . IS NOT A BORN FRENCHWOMAN.

9

:EXITS.:

FLOR.

:YAWNING: STREDELOW IS TOO PHLEGMATIC FOR A FIGHT. :YAWNS: I
SHALL DIE OF ENNUI . . . THERE IS NO GETTING A SENSATION OUT OF
ANYBODY. IF CAROJAC WOULD MAKE LOVE TO ME NOW-- THERE MIGHT BE
SOME FUN IN THAT-- BUT BROWN HAS THE GOUT-- AND HE'S TOO OLD FOR A
ROW-- IT'S VERY STUPID.

LISETTE.

:ENTERING R. C.: THE COUNT DE CAROJAC. :EXITS.:
:ENTER COUNT C. R.:

FLOR.

OH, SO DELIGHTED TO SEE YOU.

CAR.

:DOWN R. C.: MADAME BROWN, I AM SURPRISED--

FLOR.

AND SORRY TO FIND ME HERE-- I KNOW IT.

CAR.

I AM TOO POLITE TO CONTRADICT A LADY.

FLOR.

:GOING UP L. C.: YOU ARE AS POLISHED AS A RAZOR AND JUST AS SHARP.

CAR.

THANK YOU.

FLOR.

:CROSSES TO PICTURE.: WELL, THERE'S THE PICTURE. I HOPE ITS BEAU-
TY WILL CONSOLE YOU FOR THE LOSS OF THE ORIGINAL.

CAR.

I DO NOT UNDERSTAND . . . .

FLOR.

OH YES-- YOU DO. SHE GAVE YOU THE MITTEN.

10

CAR.
THE MITTEN-- ZEE GLOVES WITHOUT FINGERS-- WHAT IS THAT-- EH.

FLOR.
MR. ROUTLEDGE WAS TOO MUCH FOR YOU IN NEW YORK-- BETTER MAKE GOOD
USE OF YOUR TIME NOW-- FOR HE HAS JUST ARRIVED IN PARIS-- AND
MAY TURN THE JOKE AGAINST YOU ONCE MORE.

CAR.
[SUPPRESSING VEXATION.] MR. ROUTLEDGE IS IN PARIS-- EH? [ASIDE]
IF HE JOKE WITH ME HERE HE MAY HAVE TO PAY FOR THE JOKE. [GOES
TO PORTRAIT] THERE IS MUCH MELANCHOLY IN THE FACE.

FLOR.
[WATCHING HIM] SHE'S PONDERING O'ER THE PAST-- THE RIDES IN THE
PARK-- YOU KNOW. [LAUGHS.]

CAR.
THEY MOCK ZEMSELVES OF ME-- ALTOGETHER, SAC . . . .

FLOR.
[LAUGHING]. NOW DON'T BE ANGRY. MRS. STREPELOW WILL BE HERE IN A
MOMENT-- MAKE LOVE TO HER PICTURE-- I MUST GO TO THE PRINCE DE
BROWNE-- AND PUT A HANDKERCHIEF OVER HIS OLD HEAD OR HE WILL MAKE
UP SNEEZING. [RUNS OFF L. H. C. E. RE-APPEARS LISTENING]

CAR.
[BEFORE PORTRAIT] THE LAUGH IS GONE FROM THE FACE NOW-- I LIKE
IT SO MUCH THE BETTER . . . I DID LOVE HER-- I THINK I LOVE HER
STILL . . [ENTER LILL.] SHE IS BEAUTIFUL! HOW LOVELY IS THE
POISE OF THE HEAD, THE OUTLINE OF THE FACE . . . .

LILL.
[COMING FORWARD.] I BEG PARDON, COUNT!

CAR.
AH! MADAME-- I WAS ADMIRING . . . .

FLOR.
[PEEPING IN AND LAUGHING.] THE POISE OF THE HEAD-- THE OUTLINES OF
THE FACE. [CROSSES TO C.] LILLIAN SMILES.]

11

CARO.

[L.] ZA! LAUGH AT ME AGAIN!

FLOR.

BETTER TRANSFER YOUR DEVOTION TO ME. COUNT.

CAR.

I'LL DO ANY PENANCE FOR MY INDISCRETION-- EVEN THAT [ASIDE.]
ZEE SHE-DEVIL!

LISETTE.

[ANNOUNCING] M. DE MONTVILLAIS.
[EXITS, AS DE MONTVILLAIS ENTERS]

MONT.

[GENERAL BOW.] DELIGHTED I AM SURE.

LILL.

IT IS KIND OF YOU TO COME-- AND GIVE US THE BENEFIT OF THE ACUMEN
OF SO CELEBRATED A CRITIC.

MONT.

[CROSSING TO L.] AT PICTURE.] SO IT IS FINISHED. [EXAMINES PIC-
TURE AFFECTEDLY.] MM. AH-- YES! FINE FEELING! LE RABITEAU'S USU-
AL PRECISION OF DRAWING, LACKS TENDERNESS IN THE FLESH TINTS--
RICHLY TONED-- VERY.

FLOR.

WE KNOW ALL ABOUT IT-- NOW-- [GLANCING AT CAR.] YOU FRENCH GENTLE-
MEN ARE SUCH EXCELLENT JUDGES OF PICTURES-- EH-- COUNT?

CAR.

[SUPPRESSING VEXATION] YES-- IN ART AS IN THE POLITESSE OF LIFE
ZEE FRENCH ARE THE GREEKS OF OUR DAY.

[STRED. ENTERING R. 1. E.]

STRED.

AND THE OUTER WORLD BARGAIN-- EH. [SHAKING HANDS WITH CAR. AND
MONT.

MONT.

NOT EXACTLY THAT-- BUT . . . .

STRED.

:CROSSING TO C.: SOMETHING VERY LIKE IT-- BUT LILLIAN, I FORGOT
TO TELL YOU THAT YOUR OLD FRIEND AND PLAYMATE ARRIVED IN PARIS
YESTERDAY-- ON HIS WAY BACK TO ROME. I PREVAILED ON HIM TO STAY
OVER A DAY AND GIVE US AT LEAST ONE CALL.

LILL.

WHO?

STRED.

MR. HAROLD ROUTLEDGE-- I SHOULD THINK MR. ROUTLEDGE'S SUCCESS AS
AN ARTIST A FAIR REPLY TO M. DE CAROJAC'S CONTEMPT OF ALL ART BUT
FRENCH ART.

LILL.

:AT FIREPLACE R. WITH SUPPRESSED EMOTION: IS HAROLD-- IS MR.
ROUTLEDGE HERE?

LISETTE.

:ANNOUNCING.: M. ROUTLEDGE.

:EXIT.:

STRED.

:MEETS ROUTLEDGE SHAKES HANDS.: THIS IS KIND OF YOU MR. ROUTLEDGE.

FLOR.

:GOING TO HIM.: I AM VERY GLAD TO SEE YOU, HAROLD. :SHAKES HANDS:

ROUTLEDGE.

:ADVANCING.: MRS. STRED-- STREDLOW.

LILL.

MR. ROUTLEDGE.

FLOR.

:LAUGHING.: MRS. STREDLOW-- MR. ROUTLEDGE-- WHY DON'T YOU SHAKE
HANDS. :THEY SHAKE HANDS.:

13

LILL.

I AM GLAD YOU DID NOT PASS THROUGH PARIS WITHOUT CALLING ON US, MR. ROUTLEDGE.

ROUT.

YOU ARE VERY KIND MADAME [TO CAR.] AH COUNT DE CAROJAC.

CAR.

MR. ROUTLEDGE.

STREB.

[TO ROUT.] M. DE MONTVILLAIS-- I BEG YOUR PARDON-- HE IS SO CELE-BRATED A CRITIC THAT I SUPPOSED YOU ALREADY KNEW HIM.

ROUT.

I HAD NOT THE PLEASURE.

MONT.

I KNOW MR. ROUTLEDGE-- BY REPUTATION. I HAD THE HONOR TO CRITI-CISE HIS DANTE AND BEATRICIE NOW IN THE SALON-- IN MY PRIVATE CA-PACITY I MAY SAY HERE IN CONFIDENCE IT IS A NOBLE WORK-- FAULTLESS, OF COURSE I COULD NOT SAY THAT IN PUBLIC, YOU KNOW.

ROUT.

[SMILING AT MONT.] I SHALL RESPECT YOUR CONFIDENCE MONSIEUR.

CAR.

[MEANINGLY ON PIANO STOOL] I SEE ZEE PICTURE AND LIKE ALL PARIS I RECOGNIZE THE ORIGINAL OF THE BEATRICIE. IT MUST BE UNPLEASANT FOR MAD. STREBELOW-- VERY UNFORTUNATE.

ROUT.

14

CAR.
AH THE MEMORY MUST OFTEN BE AN ANNOYANCE TO ZEE ARTIST-- EH? MIX-
ING THE DISAPPOINTMENTS OF ZEE PAST WITH ZEE HOPES OF ZEE FUTURE.

ROUT.
{QUICKLY.} NOT IN THIS CASE, SIR. THE SUGGESTION . . .

CAR.
AH IT IS MORE THAN A SUGGESTION-- IT REALLY MIGHT BE ACCEPTED AS
A PORTRAIT OF MAD. STREDELOW.

STREB.
{LOOKING AT PICTURE. TO ROUT.} THEN YOU HAVE BEEN MORE SUCCESS-
FUL THAN LE RABITEAU, HERE-- {POINTING TO PICTURE} COMPLETED BUT
YESTERDAY-- INDEED OUR LITTLE CONCLAVE TO DAY WAS TO PASS UPON ITS
MERITS.

ROUT.
{CROSSING TO HIM.} RABITEAU IS AN EXCELLENT ARTIST.

STREB.
PERHAPS, SO. BUT IN THIS CASE HE HAS SEEMED INSPIRED WITH A SPIRIT
OF SADNESS.

CAR.
{AT ROUT.} WITH HIM IT COULD NOT HAVE BEEN MEMORY.

MONT.
{DOWN C.} I DO NOT KNOW ABOUT THAT. YOU RECOLLECT THE SCANDAL
CAUSED BY HIS PICTURE OF THE YOUNG MARQUISE DE PAULIAC?

FLOR.
{CROSSES TO R.C.} A SCANDAL ABOUT A MARQUIS-- OH DO TELL IT.
{STRED COMES DOWN L. H.}

MONT.
{C.} IT IS SAID RABITEAU FELL IN LOVE WITH HER DURING HER SITTINGS-
AND SHE WITH HIM. BUT THEY VERY PROPERLY MARRIED HER TO A RICH
OLD NODLEMAN INSTEAD OF TO A POOR ARTIST. RABITEAU HAD HIS REVENGE
HE BESTOWED UPON HER FACE AN EXPRESSION THAT SEEMED TO TELL THE
STORY.

FLOR.

{EAGERLY.} WHAT STORY?

MONT.

THE STORY OF A BROKEN HEART, OF A WOMAN BEARING IN HER BOSOM A
SECRET THAT MUST NOT LIVE YET CANNOT DIE-- A SADDER STORY THAN
THAT OF THE SPARTAN BOY WHO LET THE CUB EAT HIS HEART E'RE HE
WOULD REVEAL ITS GUILTY PRESENCE BENEATH HIS TUNIC. SOME MEMORY
OF THIS MAY HAVE GUIDED RADITEAU'S PENCIL . . . . SUGGESTED BY A
PASSING LOOK ON MRS. STREBELOW'S FACE-- A LOOK OF SORROW AT THE
PREMATURE CRUSHING OF A NEW BONNET, PERHAPS WHICH MEMORY IDEALIZED.

{FLORENCE GOES TO LILLIAN. ROUTLEDGE AND
LILLIAN'S EYES MEET SHE TURNS AWAY HER
HEAD.}

STREB.

{SEEING ALL THIS.} AND YOU THINK MRS. STREBELOW'S FACE SUGGESTED
HIS OWN EXPERIENCE?

MONT.

PERHAPS. AS A CHILD SEES FACES IN THE CLOUDS. {GOING UP.}

STREB.

TUT! TUT! LET US TO THE SMOKING ROOM. {TO LILL.} MR. ROUTLEDGE
WILL TELL YOU THE LATEST FASHIONABLE NEWS FROM NEW YORK. COME GEN-
TLEMEN. {EXIT BY MONT.}

FLOR.

AND I WILL RETURN TO BROWN. I AM AFRAID THE HANDKERCHIEF HAS FAL-
LEN OFF HIS OLD HEAD. I'M A MOTHER TO BROWNE.

{EXIT FLOR. FIRST CAR. LAST. AS HE PASSES
ROUTLEDGE, CAR. STOPS AND IN LOW TONES.}

CAR.

{TO ROUT.} AN EXCELLENT OPPORTUNITY TO REFRESH YOUR MEMORY FOR
FUTURE INSPIRATIONS . . .

ROUT.

I DO NOT UNDERSTAND . . .

16

CAB.

{BOWING.} I SHALL BE HAPPY TO GIVE THE EXPLANATION WHEN AND WHERE
YOU WILL-- {BOWS EXITS. R. U. E. TO LILL.} MADAME!

LILL.

MR. ROUTLEDGE--

ROUT.

MADAME.

LILL.

MY HUSBAND TELLS ME YOU HAVE JUST RETURNED FROM THE UNITED STATES
BUT PRAY BE SEATED.
                              {ROUT. BRINGS CHAIR L. C. BOTH SIT.}

ROUT.

MY FIRST VISIT TO AMERICA IN SEVEN YEARS. DURING THAT TIME I
SCARCELY EVER LEFT ROME.

LILL.

THE REPUTATION YOU HAVE ACQUIRED IS PROOF OF THE GOOD USE YOU HAVE
MADE OF YOUR TIME.
                              {AWKWARD PAUSE.}

LILL.

{WITH THE AIR OF ONE WHO HAS MADE UP HER MIND TO DO SOMETHING SHE
FEARED} MR. ROUTLEDGE . . . I AM GLAD TO HAVE THIS OPPORTUNITY TO
REFER TO A SUBJECT, THE . . THE DELICACY OF WHICH TIME HAS IN . . .
IN SOME DEGREE . . . LESSENED.

ROUT.

REALLY MADAME, I AM AT A LOSS TO UNDERSTAND . . . WHAT IN THE
PAST CAN REQUIRE ANY EXPLANATION BETWEEN US. WHEN YOU CLOSED
THAT PAST, YOU EXPLAINED IT.

LILL.

NO-- SIR, NOR COULD I THEN TRUST MYSELF TO DO SO. I FEEL NOW--
HAVE NEVER CEASED TO FEEL THAT . . . THE EXPLANATION IS DUE TO
YOU . . .

17

ROUT.
[RISING.] I DO NOT FEEL SO-- NOW.

LILL.
[POSITIVELY.] THEN SIR IT IS DUE TO ME . . . . AND IN JUSTICE TO
ME, I AM SURE YOU WILL HEAR IT.

ROUT.
[RISING.] I DO NOT FEEL SO-- NOW.

LILL.
[POSITIVELY.] THEN SIR IT IS DUE TO ME . . . . AND IN JUSTICE TO
ME, I AM SURE YOU WILL HEAR IT.

ROUT.
[INCLINING HIS HEAD.] MADAME . . . .

LILL.
YOU AND I WERE ENGAGED TO BE MARRIED,

ROUT.
[STANDING C.] I THOUGHT SO.

LILL.
AFTER OUR FOOLISH QUARREL-- I SENT FOR YOU TO RETURN TO ME--

ROUT.
SO I UNDERSTOOD THE LETTER. I RECEIVED FROM MRS. HOLCOMB. IN
OBEDIENCE TO THAT LETTER I DID RETURN-- I RETURNED FULL OF JOY
OF HOPE-- OF HAPPINESS-- WHEN MY HEART WAS AT ITS FULLEST-- I WAS
DISCARDED THROUGH THE MOUTH OF A LACKEY.

LILL.
AND YOU NEVER KNEW WHY? NEVER GUESSED WHY?

ROUT.
[BITTERLY.] YOU ARE MISTAKEN-- I KNEW THE VERY NEXT DAY, I
KNEW WHY WHEN I HEARD FROM MRS. HOLCOMB THAT YOU HAD ACCEPTED THE
HAND OF MR. STREBELOW WHO IS A VERY RICH MAN.

⁘

18

LILL.

BUT YOU ... NOT KNOW WHY I ACCEPTED HIM.

ROUT.

[BITTERLY STILL.] BECAUSE, AS I SAID, HE IS A VERY RICH MAN.

LILL.

[RISING.] MR. ROUT ... THAT IS TRUE.

ROUT.

YOU SEE, MADAME-- NO EXPLANATION WAS NEEDED.

LILL.

NO EXPLANATION-- I COULD THEN MAKE-- BUT MR. STREDELOW AND MYSELF
HAVE NOW BEEN MARRIED AND BEEN HAPPY TOGETHER FOR SEVEN YEARS-- AND
I CAN I BELIEVE WITHOUT INJUSTICE TO HIM EXPLAIN WHY I DID MARRY
HIM, FOR HIS MONEY-- I STATE IT PLAINLY AND TRULY.

ROUT.

I HAVE NO DOUBT THE PURITY OF YOUR MOTIVES EQUALED THE FRANKNESS
OF THE CONFESSION.

LILL.

THOSE MOTIVES I THINK IT JUST TO YOU TO STATE, DUE TO MYSELF TO
MAKE CLEAR [INVITES HIM TO R. C. SHE SITS R.H] TEN MINUTES AFTER
WITH HIS CONSENT AUNT FANNY WROTE YOU TO RETURN-- MY FATHER TOLD ME
HE WAS RUINED-- THAT IN HIS RUIN WAS INVOLVED THE RUIN OF HUNDREDS
OF OTHERS WHO HAD TRUSTED THEIR ALL TO HIM, HE BROUGHT ME TO SAVE
HIS NAME FROM INFAMY . . . SPOKE OF THE CURSES OF THE POOR, DREW
SO APPALLING A PICTURE-- THAT IN PITY-- IN FEAR-- SCARCE KNOWING
WHAT I DID. I CONSENTED-- BEFORE I HAD TIME EVEN TO THINK OF WHAT
I HAD DONE-- MR. STREDELOW CAME-- AND I ACCEPTED HIM-- I HAD
SCARCELY DONE SO WHEN YOU CALLED . . . [RISING] I . . I TRIED TO
GO TO YOU OPEN . . I TRIED . . I COULD NOT AID SO . . SO . .

ROUT.

[RISING.] SENT THAT MESSAGE WHICH CONDEMNED MY HEART TO THE BIT-
TERNESS OF ISOLATION FOREVER!

LILL.

CAN YOU FORGIVE ME?   [CROSSES TO C.]

19

ROUT.

I HAVE ALREADY DONE SO-- AND YOU ARE HAPPY?

LILL.

I AM CONTENT. AND YOU HAROLD--

ROUT.

I SUFFERED MUCH, FOR I LOVED MUCH. HAD I LOVED LESS THE WOUND TO
MY PRIDE WOULD HAVE HEALED MORE QUICKLY.

LILL.

BUT YOU ARE HAPPY NOW, SAY YOU ARE-- SAY IT.

ROUT.

LILLIAN I WOULD NOT ADD TO THE BURDEN YOU HAVE BORNE, THE WEIGHT OF
A SINGLE REPROACH. BUT I CANNOT SAY WHAT YOU ASK ME. {UP C.}
WORK AS I MAY-- DO WHAT I WILL, THE FEELING OF THE PAST CLING TO
ME. IT TINGES MY EVERY THOUGHT STEALS INTO MY EVERY CANVASS--
MAKES THE PRESENT WEARISOME-- ROBS THE FUTURE OF EVERY RAINBOW
TINT THAT MAKES WORK A CONSOLATION.

LILL.

OH HAROLD, DON'T DON'T!

ROUT.

I SHOULD NOT SAY THIS TO YOU LILLIAN, BUT I-- HAVE SUFFERED SO--
CHERISHING A SECRET I DARE NOT TELL-- AND BROODING OVER A LOVE THAT
WOULD NOT DIE . . . {FALLS IN O CHAIR L. C.}

LILL.

{WEEPING GOES TO HIM.} POOR HAROLD!

ROUT.

{PUTS ONE ARM AROUND HER WAIST} AND YOU HAVE NOT FORGOTTEN ME--
LILLIAN?

LILL.

I HAVE NEVER CEASED TO SYMPATHIZE WITH THE SORROW I KNEW-- I FELT--
YOU WERE SUFFERING . . . FOR I KNEW WHAT IT COST ME TO INFLICT IT
UPON YOU.

20

ROUT.

[MADLY--RISING.] AND YOU-- YOU LOVE ME STILL?

LILL.

[STARTING BACK.] THIS IS CRUEL OF YOU-- UNKIND HAROLD.

ROUT.

[CATCHING HER AGAIN] I KNOW NOT WHAT I SAY-- WHAT I DO-- LET ME
CARRY AWAY WITH ME SOME WORD OF AFFECTION-- SOME--

LILL.

[BREAKING FROM HIM;] LEAVE WITH ME UNTAINTED THE RESPECT I HAVE
ALWAYS ENTERTAINED FOR YOU-- HAROLD I WAS FOOLISH THUS TO TRUST
YOU-- TO TRUST MYSELF.

ROUT.

[FOLLOWING HER.] YOU SHALL-- YOU MUST . . . .

LILL.

I MUST REMEMBER WHAT YOU SEEM TO FORGET-- THAT I AM THE WIFE OF
JOHN STREBELOW-- ONE WORD MORE AND I RING-- [HAND ON BELL ON TABLE.
[ENTER CARDJAC R. D.]

CAR.

I THOUGHT SO! YOU NEED NOT RING MADAME. NO SCANDAL.
[LILL SCREAMS-- HANGS HER HEAD.]

ROUT.

SIR!

CAR.

[TO LILL.] MR. ROUTLEDGE'S MEMORY OF WHERE HE STANDS WILL CALM
THE ARDOR OF HIS INSPIRATIONS.

[ROUTLEDGE BOWS. COUNT BOWS.]

C U R T A I N.

---:0:---

---:0:---

S E T

VESTIBULE AND STAIRWAY OF THE AMERICAN
EMBASSY AT PARIS.   GUESTS GOING UP AND
COMING DOWN STAIRS.
SERVANTS COMING DOWN STAIRS FROM L. OF-
FICE R. U. E. STREBELOW AND CAROJAC FROM
CLOAK ROOM R. U. E. TO C. FRENCH OFFICER
AND LADY. ENTER R. 3. E. GO OFF R. U. E.
SERVANT FROM R. U. E. GOES UP STAIRS AND
OFF L. U. E. WITH CARD.

CAR.

MAD. STREBELOW IS WITH YOU THIS EVENING, OF COURSE.

STRED.

SHE WILL BE DOWN PRESENTLY. YOU FREQUENTLY HONOR OUR RECEPTION
AT THE AMERICAN LEGATION M. LE COUNTE.

CAR.

THE AMERICAN LADIES ARE SO VERY BEAUTIFUL.

STRED.

AND IN THE PRESENCE OF FEMALE BEAUTY, A FRENCH GENTLEMAN IS NEVER
BLIND, EH M. LE COUNTE? {LAUGHS.}
{ENTER FLORENCE R. U. E. DOWN STAIRS.}

FLOR.

MR. STREBELOW, YOU ARE LATE   HOW IS LILLIAN THIS EVENING?   M. LE
COUNTE {NODS.}

CARO.

MADAME.

STRED;

{R. H.} MRS. STREBELOW WAS DETAINED WITH HER DAUGHTER.

FLOR.

{C.} LILLIAN IS A SLAVE TO THAT CHILD. {LOOKING R. U. E.} WHY
HERE COMES THE PRINCE, I JUST LEFT HIM ON THE SOFA IN THE BACK HALL
ROOM, TALKING TO MRS. GORDON; I THOUGHT I'D GOT HIM FIXED FOR TWO
HOURS AT LEAST.

{FRENCH OFFICER ENTERS FROM CLOAK ROOM,
GOES UP STAIRS AND OFF L. U. E. THEN SER-
VANT COMES FROM L. U. E, EXITS INTO CLOAK
ROOM. ENTER BROWN L. 2. E, BOBBLING WITH
A CANE.}

BROWN.

{CROSSING TO FLOR.} AH . . YOU ARE HERE, MY DEAR . . HE EH. YOU
LOST ME-- DIDN'T YOU? HE, EH, {PATTING HER UNDER THE CHIN} I
HAVE BEEN TALKING WITH YOUNG MRS. GORDON, MY DEAR, YOU MUSTN'T BE
JEALOUS. I I'M NOT A DON JUAN MY LOVE, I'M NOT A DON JUAN {CROSSES
TO STRED. LAUGHS.} I SAY STREDELOW, OLD BOY. {APART TO STRED.
WHO HAS CROSSED TO R. C. FLORENCE TALKS WITH CAROJAC.} THESE
YOUNG WOMAN ARE JEALOUS CREATURES {LAUGHS} THEY KEEP THEIR EYES
ON THEIR HUSBANDS, {LAUGHS.} IT'S FUN TO TEASE THEM NOW AND THEN
{LAUGHS, POKES STRED. IN THE SIDE.} ISN'T IT? JUST FOR A LITTLE
SPICE, YOU KNOW! IT'S WICKED I KNOW IT'S WICKED. BUT {LAUGHS}
I DO BELIEVE THEY LOVE A MAN ALL THE MORE FOR A TOUCH OF-- OF DEV-
ILTRY-- NOW AND THEN-- YOU KNOW.

{GENTLEMEN ENTER R. D. EXIT INTO ARCH
ROOM AFTER GLANCING AT BROBNE AND LOOKING
ABOUT AS IF NEW TO HIM.}

FLOR.

{TO CAROJAC.} WAIT TILL I GET BROWN FIXED NICE AND COMFORTABLE
SOMEWHERE MY DEAR-- DON'T YOU WANT TO COME INTO THE NEXT ROOM--
THERE'S A SOFA AND AN EASY CHAIR-- WE'LL HAVE A NICE VISIT YOU AND
I-- ALL BY OURSELVES.

{GENTLEMAN AND LADY ENTER R. D. GO TO-
WARDS CLOAK ROOM SERVANT ENTERS WITH
SALVER FROM CLOAK ROOM, GENT PLACES HIS
CARD ON IT, SERVANT GOES UP AND OFF L.U.E.
GENT AND LADY INTO CLOAK ROOM.}

BROWN.

{LAUGHS.} YES, MY DEAR-- I SAY STREDELOW A LITTLE J ALOUS-- DO
YOU SEE? SHE LIKES TO BE ALONE WITH ME. COME, MY LOVE {GOING WITH

FLORENCE, LOOKS BACK AT STREBELOW.⦂ TRY IT STREBELOW-- TRY IT
WITH YOUR WIFE-- IT WORKS TO A CHARM-- A LITTLE DEVILTRY, YOU
KNOW: A TRIFLE JEALOUS, EH, FLORENCE. TRY IT STREBELOW, COME, MY
LOVE. I'M NOT A DON JUAN, MY DEAR, I'M NOT A DON JUAN.
⦂EXITS L. 2. E.⦂

FLOR.
⦂HER FINGER TO HER LIPS⦂ SH! I'LL HAVE THE PRINCE ASLEEP ON THE
SOFA IN LESS THAN FIVE MINUTES.
⦂THE COUNT BOWS AND WAIVES HIS HAND-- SHE
RETURNS IT, EXITS AFTER BROWN. ENTER
MONTVILLAIS R. 2. E.⦂

MONT.
GOOD EVENING, GENTLEMEN, DROPPED IN AT THE OPERA THIS EVENING.
ORTALINI'S VOICE'S SPLENDID-- BUT THE CHORUS EXECRABLE. AH, A
NEW BIT OF BRONZE SINCE THE LAST RECEPTION-- HYMAN-- RATHER TOO
FULL ABOUT THE TORSO.
⦂ENTER GEO. WASHINGTON PHIPPS, R. 2. E.
HE IS CROSSING THE STAGE RAPIDLY STOPS
SUDDENLY, HE IS AN ENERGETIC YOUNG AMERICAN
BUSINESS MAN IN MANNER AND APPEARANCE--
DRESS SUIT.⦂

PHIPPS.
EH-- STREBELOW!

STRED.
MR. PHIPPS.

PHIPPS.
⦂CROSSING TO STRED⦂ GLAD TO SEE YOU, HEARD YOU WERE LIVING HERE.
HOW'S YOUR WIFE.
⦂GENTLEMEN AND LADY ENTER FROM CLOAK ROOM
GO UP AND OFF L. U. E. SERVANT COMES
DOWN FROM L. U. E. AND EXITS TO CLOAK ROOM⦂

STRED.
WELL, THANK YOU, WHEN DID YOU ARRIVE IN PARIS?

                              PHIPPS.
THIS EVENING, HALF PAST SEVEN TRAIN. PARIS IS A VERY PRETTY CITY,
STREETS WELL LIGHTED: MAGNIFICENT OPERA HOUSE. THE INSIDE IS PAR-
TICULARLY GORGEOUS: DROPPED INTO THE PALAIS ROYAL ON THE WAY.
THE COMEDIE FRANSAZE IS CONSIDERABLY LARGER. BUT THE OPERA COMECK--

                              MONT.
[SUDDENLY.] PARDON MONSIEUR-- PARDON!

                              PHIPPS.
[LOOKS AT MONT. THEN AT STREB.] FRIEND OF YOURS?

                              STREB.
M. MONTVILLAIS: A FELLOW TOWNSMAN, MR. PHIPPS, OF NEW YORK CITY.

                              PHIPPS.
C. WASHINGTON PHIPPS-- DRY GOODS.

                              MONT.
DRY GOODS?

                              PHIPPS.
57 CHURCH STREET.

                              MONT.
87?

                              PHIPPS.
[TO STREBELOW POINTING BACK AT MONT. WITH HIS THUMB] WHAT LINE?

                              STREB.
STATIONARY.

                              PHIPPS.
AH.

PHIPPS.

[TO STREB.] SAME BUSINESS?

STREB.

[R. C.] CUTLERY AND FIRE-ARMS.

PHIPPS.

OH.

MONT.

YOUR PARDON, MR. PHIPPS, I OWE YOU AN APOLOGY FOR HAVING INTER-
RUPTED YOUR REMARKS. PARDON BUT YOU HAVE BEEN TO THE GRAND OPERA--
AND TO THE PALAIS ROYAL-- AND THE COMEDIE FRANCAISE AND THE OPERA
COMIQUE-- AND YOU ARRIVED IN THE CITY OF PARIS AT HALF PAST SEVEN
THIS EVENING.

CAR.

YOU HAVE SEEN CONSIDERABLE OF THE METROPOLIS, MR. PHIPPS DURING
YOUR COMPARATIVELY SHORT VISIT.

PHIPPS.

NOT AS MUCH AS I HAD HOPED TO SEE BY THIS TIME. I HAVE BEEN IN
THE CITY OF PARIS FOUR HOURS. DELAYED AT THE GRAND HOTEL. IT
TOOK ME AT LEAST FIFTEEN MINUTES, SIR, TO PERSUADE THE CHAMBERMAID
THAT BROUGHT ME THE CANDLES, THAT I DID NOT REQUIRE HER PRESENCE,
WHILE I WAS CHANGING MY TRAVELING SUIT FOR A DRESS COAT AND BLACK
PANTALOONS. THESE FRENCH CHAMBERMAIDS ARE SLOW TO TAKE A HINT--
IN THAT DIRECTION. THE TUILERIES, BY THE WAY, PRESENT A RATHER IM-
POSING APPEARANCE IN THE SNOW AND MOONLIGHT. I HAD THE DRIVER GO
ROUND BY THE WAY OF THE TUILERIES AND THE PALACE OF THE LOUVRE
ON THE WAY TO THE LEGATION. THE ARK DEE TRIUMPH IS RATHER NEAT IN
ITS WAY; WHEN WE GOT INTO THE CHAMPS ELIZA, I TOLD THE DRIVER TO
TAKE A HALF-HOUR'S TURN TO THE ARK, AND WE CAME BACK BY THE WAY OF
THE FOURRG ST. HONORY AND THE CHURCH DEE ST. PHILIPEE. TOURISTS,
GENERALLY LOSE A GREAT DEAL OF TIME UNNECESSARILY. I'VE GOT EVERY
THING I WANT TO SEE IN PARIS WRITTEN DOWN IN MY NOTE BOOK. BOUGHT
A GUIDE TO PARIS IN LONDON. [TAKES A SMALL GUIDE BOOK FROM POCKET]
PRONUNCIATION ALL SPELT OUT IN ENGLAND-- CARRY A MAP OF THE CITY
IN MY COAT POCKET.

[TAKES OUT MAP LOOKS AT IT, ENTER ENGLISH
OFFICER AND GENTLEMAN WITH LADY FROM D.
EXIT INTO CLOAK ROOM.]

STREB.

WHEN DID YOU LEAVE NEW YORK? MR. PHIPPS?

PHIPPS.

NOVEMBER THIRTEEN-- TWO O'CLOCK P.M. ARRIVED IN LIVERPOOL NOVEMBER
TWENTY THIRD, HALF PAST TEN A. M. EXACTLY ONE WEEK AND A HALF AGO.
SPENT FOUR DAYS AND A HALF IN THE CITY OF LONDON AND VICINITY.
I SAW LONDON THOROUGHLY.

MONT.

VOILA L. AMERICAN! HE'LL SEE ALL PARIS IN A FORTNIGHT.

PHIPPS.

I SHALL BE IN PARIS PRECISELY THREE DAYS. DETAINED TILL FRIDAY
ON BUSINESS,-- FIGURED SILKS. I SHALL THEN RUN OVER TO SWITZERLAND.
THEY TELL ME I CAN SEE MONT. BLANC FROM THE WINDOWS OF THE HOTEL
AT GENEVA.

CAR.

MON, DIEU!

PHIPPS.

THAT WILL SAVE CONSIDERABLE TIME. BERLIN, BY THE WAY, IS A VERY
BEAUTIFUL CITY, WIDE STREETS, CAME FROM LONDON BY THE WAY OF BER-
LIN, REMAINED THERE THIRTY SIX HOURS-- MISSED A TRAIN, DELAYED
FIVE HOURS, STOPPED OVER AT DRESDEN, ON THE ROUTE FROM BERLIN, AND
AT COLOGNE, BIG CATHEDRAL, BONES OF ELEVEN THOUSAND VIRGINS, IN
THE CHURCH OF ST. URSULA, I DIDN'T COUNT 'EM, BUT MY GUIDE SWORE
TO THE FACT, HE WOULDN'T LET UP ON A BID, GUIDES NEVER LIE, IN
EUROPE.

MONT.

YOU VISITED THE DRESDEN GALLERY, MONSIEUR, YOU ADMIRE WORKS OF
ARTS.

PHIPPS.

YES, I LIKE PICTURES, I SPENT NEARLY TWENTY MINUTES IN THE GALLERY
AT DRESDEN.

MONT.

DIABLE!

PHIPPS.

O REVOIR, GENTLEMAN, AS YOU FRENCHMAN SAY, SEE YOU AGAIN STREBELOW,
MY REGARDS TO YOUR WIFE ¡GOING R, HAND ... RD TO ATTENDANT¡ THERE'S
MY CARD, SIR G. WASHINGTON PHIPPS, N.Y. U. S. A.

¡EXITS L, UPSTAIRS PRECEDED BY SERVANT.
PHIPPS RUNS UP STAIRS 2 STEPS AT A TIME IN
RUSHING OFF R. H. SERVANT CALLS, THIS
WAY SIR POINTING L. U. E. PHIPPS ''OH
ALL RIGHT'' BOUNDS UP THE STAIRS L. U. E.¡

STRED.

WHATEVER FAULTS MY COUNTRYMEN MAY HAVE, GENTLEMAN-- YOU ITH OWN
THAT LASTING TIME IS NOT ONE OF THEM.

CAR.

OUI, MON AMI, C'EAT VRAI, CES'T VRAI. ¡MOVING TO ..C.¡

MONT.

BOOM-- WHIZ-- CHICK! MR. PHIPPS IS A BULLET. HE IS HERE AND HE
IS GONE.

¡ENTER LILL, THROUGH ARCH R. U.E.¡

STRED.

MY WIFE-- ¡GOES TO HER.¡ BUT WHERE'S YOUR FATHER DEAR?

LILL.

NATALIE INSISTED HE SHOULD RETURN TO HER. HE SAID HE FELT TOO
TIRED FOR A FORMAL RECEPTION LIKE THIS-- BUT WOULD PERHAPS CALL AT
A CIRCLE TO SEE AN OLD NEW YORK FRIEND. IN WHICH CASE HE WILL NOT
BE HOME TILL LATE ¡SEEING MONT¡ AH M. MONTVILLAIS, ¡THEY BOW¡ SHE
TAKES STREBELOW'S ARM.¡ COME, LET US MAKE ONE BOW UP STAIRS AND
RETURN HOME.

¡GOING UP C. THEY PASS CAROJAC, ROUTLEDGE
IS SEEN COMING DOWN STAIRS.¡

STRED.

¡UP C.¡ YOU OVERLOOK THE COUNT DE CAROJAC, MY DEAR.

LILL.

¡LAUGHING AND TURNING BOWS LIGHTLY.¡ SO I DID-- PARDON M, COUNT
¡COUNT BOWS.¡

ROUTLEDGE NOW ON STAGE MEETS STREB, AND
LILL. PREPARING TO GO UP STAIRS, AWKWARD
GETTING OUT OF EACH OTHER'S WAYS.

ROUT.

[ON STEPS L. C.] I BEG YOUR PARDON.

STREB.

[AT FOOT OF STEPS] I BEG YOUR PARDON. AH ROUTLEDGE GLAD TO SEE
YOU HERE.

LILL.

[BOWING FORMALLY] M. ROUTLEDGE.

ROUT.

MRS. STREBELOW--

STREB.

AND YOU STILL PERSIST IN STARTING FOR ROME TO-MORROW.

ROUT.

I MUST TAKE THE EARLY TRAIN.

STREB.

THEN WE MUST SAY GOOD BYE, THIS EVENING.

ROUT.

YES, INDEED-- GOOD BYE, SIR-- MADAME-- FAREWELL [BOWS.]
                         [STREB. AND LILL. MOUNT THE FIRST STEPS,
                         STREB. HIS WIFE ON HIS ARM TURNS SUDDENLY]
MR. ROUTLEDGE.

ROUT.

SIR?

STREB.

YOU MUST AFFORD ME OPPORTUNITY TO BID FOR YOUR DANTE AND BEATRICE .

ROUT.

PARDON ME-- BUT I DO NOT INTEND TO SELL THAT PICTURE.

STRED.

THEN AT SOME FUTURE TIME--GOOD BYE-- ONCE MORE--

ROUT.

GOOD BYE.

[EXEUNT UP STAIRS STRED, & LILL.]

ROUT. EXITS R. U. E. C ROJAC AND MONT-
VILLAIS ARE CONVERSING.]

MONT.

BUT WHY?

CAR.

BECAUSE I HATE HIM. HE MADE A LAUGHING STOCK OF ME IN NEW YORK--
HE CAME BETWEEN ME . . . AND . . .

MONT.

BUT NOT HERE . . . NOT HERE IN THE LEGATION.

CAR.

YES-- HERE AND NOW-- HE GOES AWAY TO-MORROW.
[MOVES AS IF TO APPROACH ROUT. MONT.
CATCHES HIM BY THE ARM AND DETAINS HIM.]

MONT.

YOU WILL EVOKE A SCANDAL--IT WILL BE SAID THAT MADAME STREBELOW . .
IS THE CAUSE OF THE FIGHT. YOU'VE BEEN DINING-- YOU'RE FLUSHED.

CAR.

[STILL MORE EXCITED] WHAT I CARE-- BOTH HE AND SHE HAVE ALWAYS
PROVOKED ME-- I GAVE HIM HIS CUE AT STREBELOW'S HOUSE TO DAY I
WILL GIVE HIM GOOD CAUSE TO FIGHT IF HE WILL FACE A SWORD. I'LL
TEACH THEM TO LAUGH AT ALPHONSE CAROJAC.

MONT.

WELL BUT ONE MOMENT-- COME HERE WHERE WE CAN TALK.
[DRAWS HIM OFF L. S. E.] AS THEY EXIT
FLORENCE WHO HAS BEEN LISTENING AT THE
ARCH L. U. E. SHE RUNS TO THE STAIRS DOWN
WHICH PHIPPS IS COMING.]

10

FLOR.

{ASIDE.} A SENSATION AT LAST A FIGHT-- SWORDS. THE WHOLE COLONY WILL BE ALIVE-- I MUST TELL LILLIAN--

{MEETS PHIPPS ON STAIRS.}

PHIPPS.

MRS. BROW . . . {BUS. OF DODGING EACH OTHER.}

FLOR.

DON'T STOP ME-- I'M IN A HURRY.

PHIPPS.

SO AM I-- BUT I THINK I HAVE SOMETHING TO SAY TO YOU.

FLOR.

{ON STAIRS.} WHAT IS IT?

PHIPPS.

BROWN STILL ALIVE?

FLOR.

YES.

PHIPPS.

IN GOOD HEALTH?

FLOR.

NOTHING BUT THE GOUT.

PHIPPS.

THEN I DON'T THINK I HAVE ANYTHING TO SAY-- GOOD EVENING.

{MAKES WAY FOR FLOR, WHO MAKES UP STAIRS, DISAPPEARS.}

PHIPPS.

MORE STATUTORY. AH WHAT IS THIS, HYMAN. {TAKING OUT NOTE BOOK} I THOUGHT SO-- KNEW HIM BY HISTORCH-- LET ME SEE-- {WRITING} THAT IS THE SEVENTEENTH STATUE OF HYMAN I'VE SEEN SINCE I LANDED IN LIVERPOOL. THIS ONE, I PRESUME IS DIANA, DIANA COMES UNDER THE D'S, NO. IT CAN'T BE DIANA. I HAVE NOTICED DIANA ALWAYS

11

WEARS THE MOON AS A HEAD-DRESS.   IT MUST BE VENUS-- I'LL PUT IT
IN THE V'S {WRITES{ AMERICAN LEGATION VENUS NUMBER-- I HAVE SEEN
NINETY-SEVEN VENUSES SINCE I LANDED IN LIVERPOOL-- VENUS IS MORE
POPULAR THAN HYMAN-- IN EUROPE AMERICAN LEGATION-- VENUS-- NUMBER
{LOOKS AT STATUE AGAIN{ NO, IT CAN'T BE VENUS EITHER-- TOO MANY
CLOTHES FOR VENUS. VENUS IN FULL DRESS IS NOT POPULAR-- IN EUROPE.
I'LL CALL IT JUNO. SHE GOES UNDER THE J'S. PATRONESS OF MARRIAGE
THE GUIDE BOOK SAYS-- JUNO {WRITES{ NUMBER THREE-- I'M SHORT OF
JUNO'S-- JUNO IS NOT AS POPULAR HERE AS VENUS. LET ME, SEE
{PULLS OUT MAP{ I CAN INSTRUCT THE DRIVER TO RETURN TO THE HO-
TEL BY THE WAY OF THE MADDYLEEN-- AND THE NATIONAL LIBRARY. {HOLD-
ING OUT MAP{ PERHAPS WE CAN DODGE ROUND BY THE WAY OF THE CATHE-
DRAL DEE-NOTER-DAM--

{GOES UP R. MEETS ROUTLEDGE WHO ENTERS
FROM CLOAK ROOM.{

ROUT.
AH PHIPPS, I HEARD YOU WERE HERE, ARE YOU IN A PARTICULAR HURRY--

PHIPPS.
NO I'M IN A GENERAL HURRY.

ROUT.
DO YOU KNOW THE COUNT DE CARDJAC?

PHIPPS.
THAT BLACK FELLOW IN THE CUTLERY AND FIRE ARMS LINE-- JUST BEEN
INTRODUCED {LOOKS AT HIS WATCH{ JUST NINE MINUTES AGO.

ROUT.
HE HAS BEEN TRYING TO PROVOKE ME-- ALMOST INSULTED ME TO-DAY.

PHIPPS.
PUNCH HIS HEAD.

ROUT.
HE I SEND AT A CHALLENGE TO A DUEL.

PHIPPS.
WHAT FOR?

ROUT,

COME INTO THE ANTI-ROOM. IT IS A VERY DELICATE MATTER-- THIS
PLACE IS TOO PUBLIC-- I WOULD AVOID IT IF I CAN HONORABLY {AS
THEY GO OFF R. U. E.} THE REPUTATION OF AN AMERICAN LADY IS IN-
VOLVED IN THE--

{EXIT R.U.E. THROUGH ARCH.}

FLOR,

{COMES DOWN STAIRS QUICKLY.} I CANNOT FIND HER ANYWHERE-- I'VE
BEEN THROUGH ALL THE ROOMS-- {ENTER LISETTE} AH LISETTE HAVE
YOU SEEN MRS. STREDELOW?

LISETTE,

NOT FOR A QUARTER OF AN HOUR.

FLOR,

YOU WILL FIND MR. BROWNE ASLEEP ON THE SOFA IN THE RETIRING ROOM.
PLEASE GO SIT BY HIS SIDE TILL HE WAKES UP. {LIS. GOING} STOP--
WHEN HE DOES WAKE UP TELL HIM-- THAT'S IT, I'LL GO HOME WITH LILL-
IAN-- TELL HIM HIS WIFE HAS COME-- AND SAY HE MUST GO RIGHT HOME,
AND PLEASE HELP HIM ON WITH HIS THINGS. AND, PLEASE SEE THE HAND-
KERCHIEF IS ON HIS HEAD-- AND IF HIS POOR LEG SLIPS OFF THE SOFA--
PUT IT BACK, GENTLY, SO AS NOT TO DISTURB HIM.

{LISETTE CURTSIES AND EXITS L. H.}
POOR OLD BROWNE-- I TAKE AS MUCH CARE OF HIM AS IF HE WERE A BABY.
I'VE TAKEN THE PLACE HIS OWN MOTHER OCCUPIED 75 YEARS AGO; BUT
WHERE CAN LILLIAN BE-- SHE MUST KNOW OF THIS-- I'M SURE CAROJAC
WILL DO WHAT HE THREATENED. IT WILL BE MAGNIFICENT-- IN ALL THE
PAPERS. THEY WILL HEAR OF IT IN NEW YORK-- THE HERALD WILL IN-
TERVIEW US AS A FRIEND OF THE LADY WHOSE NAME WAS INVOLVED-- WHAT
MRS. BROWNE SAYS-- WHAT MRS. BROWN THINKS-- DESCRIPTION OF THE COM-
BATANTS MRS. BROWN WIFE OF THE AMERICAN MILLIONAIRE NOW RESIDING
IN PARIS ALL IN BIG TYPE. I WONDER WHAT THEY'LL THINK OF IT ALL
ON THE AVENUE-- MRS. BROW-- THAT MUST IT HAVE! IF IT WAS ONLY
LIVINGSTON-- OR THE COUNT DE DE CROMPOTILLA. BUT WHERE CAN LIL-
LIAN BE? I MUST FIND HER.

{GO UP STAIRS QUICKLY.} ROUT ENTERS L,
WITH CAROJAC ROUT, WITH HIM-- DOWN THE
ARCH THEN ROUTE SEES PHIPPS WITH HIM.}

PHIPPS.

[TO ROUT.] YOU ARE RIGHT-- THE FELLOW MUST BE A SCOUNDREL-- FOR
STINGELOW'S SAKE AS WELL AS FOR HIS WIFE'S.

[ROUT AND PHIPPS HAVE THEIR HATS IN
THEIR HANDS-- ROUT, HAS CLOAK. PHIPPS
COAT ON HIS ARM, THEY ARE GOING OFF R.B.E]

CAR.

[L. MEANINGLY.] YOU ARE NOT RUNNING AWAY, MR. ROUTLEDGE?

ROUT.

[STOPPING SHORT] NOT FROM YOU M. DE CAROJAC.

CAR.

WITHOUT GIVING ME THE OPPORTUNITY TO GIVE YOU THE EXPLANATION . . .

MONT.

[TO CAROJAC.]   -- CAROJAC.

CAROJAC.

[STOPPING MONT. LES GESTES] LAISSE MOI FAIRE.

ROUT.

[QUIETLY.] I THINK, J.-- I UNDERSTAND YOU WITHOUT ANY EXPLANA-
TION.

PHIPPS.

[TO ROUT, ASIDE.] THE FELLOW HAS BEEN DRINKING.

MONT.

[CROSSING TO MISEL .] P MILY M. J. ROUTL DGE TO OFFER THE EX-
PLANATION. THE COUNT IS A LITTLE IRRITATED AT THE UNFORTUNATE
R MELANC T MRS. ST. FELLOW WHICH IN YOUR BEATRICIA IS PLACED
ON PUBLIC EXHIBITION.

ROUT.

[QUIETLY.] THE WHY SHOULD THE COUNT CONCERN HIMSELF ABOUT THE
MATTER-- EH? BU-- AS A FRIEND-- AN OLD AND DEAR FRIEND OF MADAME
STINGELOW.

14

CAR.

[CROSSING TO C.] I THINK SUCH THINGS MAY BE DONE IN AMERICA--
DONE IN FRANCE THEY ARE INSOLENCE-- WHICH NO FRENCH GENTLEMAN WOULD
BE GUILTY OF TO A FRENCH LADY.

[ENTER FLOR. AND LILLIAN ON STAIRS L.U.E.]

ROUT.

[A LITTLE MORE WARMLY.] IF YOU SEEK A QUARREL, SIR, I BEG YOU
WILL FIND A CAUSE UNCONNECT D WITH THE NAME OF ANY LADY AMERICAN
OR FRENCH-- AND A PLACE IN WHICH AN AMERICAN WILL NOT IN ACCEPT-
ING IT BE FORCED TO FORGET THE RESPECT DUE TO THE FLAG UNDER
WHOSE PROTECTION YOU ARE SPEAKING--

CAR.

[INSOLENTLY.] THAT IS THE FIRST TIME I EVER HEARD THAT THE FLAG
PROTECTED ANYTHING OR ANY BODY.

MONT.

[EXPOSTULATINGLY.] CARDUJAC-- MON CHER!

PHIPPS.

[TO ROUT.] IF YOU DON'T SLAP HIS FACE, I WILL--

ROUT.

[WAVING PHIPPS BACK.] THAT FLAG PROTECTS YOU NOW.

CAR.

[STILL MORE INSOLENTLY.] I BEG YOUR PARDON-- 'TIS YOU WHO AP-
PEAL TO IT-- THE COUNT DE CARDUJAC NEEDS NEITHER THE AMERICAN RAG
NOR AN AMERICAN PETTICOAT TO PROTECT HIM.

ROUT.

[BURSTING OUT.] YOU ARE EITHER DRUNK OR A BLACKGUARD.
[FLORENCE SCREAMS.]

CAR.

[RUSHING TO ROUT.] COFFIN! YOU ARE ONE LIAR-- ONE COWARD--
[THROWS HIS GLOVE IN ROUTLEDGE'S FACE.]

PHIPPS.

[MAD WITH EXCITEMENT.] KNOCK HIM DOWN!

15

{FLORENCE SCREAMS-- AS PEOPLE RUSH OUT AT
ALL DOORS AND ON STAIRS. ROUTLEDGE
KNOCKS CAROJAC DOWN. PHIPPS MENACINGLY
FACES MONTVILLAIS. FOOTMAN CATCHES
ROUTLEDGE ONE HOLDS CAROJAC WHO RISES TO
HIS FEET. LILL. STREB. GUESTS ETC. ON
LANDING THERE IN TIME TO SEE CAROJAC
STRICKEN DOWN, WOMEN SCREAM, OLD BROWN
HANDKERCHIEF ON HEAD APPEARS AT DOOR.

C U R T A I N.

---:0:---

<u>A C T   I V .</u>

---oOo---

<u>S C E N E   I S T.</u>   : THE CURTAIN RISES ON AN EMPTY STAGE,
AFTER A FEW SECONDS OF SILENCE PROLONGED
AFTER THE APPLAUSE TO THE SCENE, ENTER
ROUTLEDGE IN CIRCULAR CLOAK, FOLLOWED
BY PHIPPS IN OVERCOAT, FROM TERRACE. :

ROUT,
: LOOKING ROUND, :   THIS IS THE SPOT,

PHIPPS.
: LOOKING ROUND, :   SOLEMN, SPLENDID, AND ICY.   : PULLS OUT WATCH, :
WHAT DO YOU CALL IT?

ROUT,
ALL THAT THE RUSSIAN BULLETS LEFT OF A ONCE ROYAL CHATEAU,

PHIPPS,
: MAKING NOTE, :   IT MAKES ME SHIVER,

ROUT,
: THOUGHTFULLY, :   HOW CALMLY THE FEVERISH CITY SEEMS TO SLEEP!
PHIPPS!   : PHIPPS COMES DOWN R,C, :   I FEEL A STRANGE SENSE OF OM-
INOUS AWE.   I FEEL AS IF I WERE DESTINED NEVER TO LEAVE THIS SPOT
ALIVE.

PHIPPS.
NONSENSE!   IT'S THE FIRST EFFECT OF THE PLACE.   YOU'LL SOON SHAKE
THAT OFF.

ROUT,
MAY BE SO,   BUT THIS MAN IS SAID TO BE THE BEST SWORDSMAN IN
EUROPE.
PHIPPS,
DO YOU KNOW NOTHING OF THE SMALL SWORD?

                    ROUT,
I AM A PRETTY FAIR SWORDSMAN;   I LEARNED ITS USE AT THE UNIVERSITY
IN GERMANY; AND IN EUROPE, NO ARTIST'S STUDIO IS COMPLETE WITHOUT
A PAIR OF FOILS.

                    PHIPPS,
: C :   I SHOULD FANCY THAT FENCING WITH FOILS FOR AMUSEMENT IS A
VERY DIFFERENT THING FROM CARRYING ON A SERIOUS DISCUSSION WITH
BUTTONLESS SWORDS.

                    ROUT,
NOT WITH ME, I THINK.   I AM GENERALLY COOLEST IN THE MOMENT OF
DANGER.   BUT BEFORE THEY COME, THERE IS ONE THING I WANT YOU TO
PROMISE ME.

                    PHIPPS,
WHAT IS IT?

                    ROUT,
THAT YOU WILL DO ALL YOU CAN TO PREVENT THE REAL CAUSE OF THIS
QUARREL FROM BEING KNOWN.   REMEMBER, I FIGHT TO AVENGE THE INSULT
TO OUR COUNTRY, SIMPLY.   FOR LILLIAN'S SAKE, FOR STREBELOW'S SAKE,
LET NO SUSPICION GET ABROAD OF --

                    PHIPP,
YOU MAY DEPEND UPON ME.

                    ROUT,
DELIBERATELY AND PERSISTENTLY THIS MAN'S JEALOUSY AND IRRITATED
VANITY HAVE FORCED THIS FIGHT, AND WHATEVER WAY IT END, I WOULD
HAVE HIS ATTEMPT TO AVENGE HIMSELF FOR HIS REJECTION BAFFLED, AS
FAR AS LILLIAN AND HER HUSBAND ARE CONCERNED.   YOU UNDERSTAND?

                    PHIPPS,
I DO.   WHAT YOU ARE DOING, I WOULD DO, THOUGH PRACTICALLY I DON'T
KNOW A REVOLVER FROM A JACK-KNIFE, OR A SMALL SWORD FROM A CORK-
SCREW, HUSH! : LISTENS: THEY ARE COMING.
                         : PAUSE, :

          : ENTER MONT. CAROJAC AND DR. WATSON.
            THEY ARE ALL IN OVERCOATS.   MONTVILLAIS
            CARRIES FOUR SMALL SWORDS.   THE DOCTOR
            A CANE, :

MONT.
: TO ROUT. & PHIPPS.: YOUR SERVANT, GENTLEMEN. YOU WILL PARDON
THE DELAY. THE SWORDS WERE AT MY APARTMENTS AND WE STOPPED ON THE
WAY FOR DR. WATSON, : BOWS ALL ROUND.: AN OLD LONDON FRIEND OF
MINE WHO WILLINGLY AGREED TO OFFER HIS PROFESSIONAL SERVICES TO
WHOEVER MAY NEED THEM.

DR. WATSON.
: TO ROUT.: PLEASED TO MAKE YOUR ACQUAINTANCE, SIR, I SHALL BE
HAPPY, BELIEVE ME, TO ATTEND YOU AS TO ATTEND MY FRIEND'S FRIEND.

PHIPPS.
HAPPY EITHER WAY -- STRICTLY IMPARTIAL.

ROUT.
: TO DOCTOR.: I THANK YOU, DOCTOR.
: DR. GOES UP.:

CARO.
: AS IF TIRED OF DELAY.: ALLONS -- MONTVILLAIS.

: MONTVILLAIS ADVANCES C. PRESENTS THE
HANDLES OF THE SWORDS TO PHIPPS, WHO
TAKES THEM LOOKS AT THEM, MOVES OVER TO
ROUTLEDGE.:

PHIPPS.
: TO ROUT.: I'M TO TAKE MY CHOICE, I BELIEVE.

ROUT.
CERTAINLY.

PHIPPS.
: STARING AT EACH SWORD IN TURN, MOVING TO C.: ABOUT THE SAME
LENGTH, APPARENTLY, : FEELS POINTS WITH HIS FINGERS, PRICKING IT :
I NEVER SAW TWO BLOTS OF BLACK MORE LIKE EACH OTHER. I SHOULDN'T
HAVE THE LEAST CHOICE AS TO WHICH OF THEM WAS PASSED THROUGH MY
BODY.
: HE REVERSES THE SWORDS, PRESENTING THE
HANDLES CROSSED TO MONTVILLIAS.:

                              : MONT TAKES ONE, PLACES THE POINT ON
                              GROUND, BENDS THE BLADES EACH WAY SEVER-
                              AL TIMES. :
                              PHIPPS WATCHING HIM IMITATES HIM WITH
                              THE OTHER SWORD. :

                    MONT.
ARE YOU SATISFIED, MR. PHIPPS?

                    PHIPPS.
PERFECTLY.   : ASIDE. :   MINE SEEMS TO BEND AS MUCH AS HIS   DOES.
                            : ROUT. AND CAROJAC TAKE OFF THEIR COATS,
                            STAND IN SHIRT SLEEVES. :

                    PHIPPS.
: TO DOCTOR. :   WON'T THIS BE A TRIFLE CHILLY. ?

                    DOCTOR.
THEY WILL BE WARM ENOUGH AFTER THEIR SWORDS ARE CROSSED.   THE
EXERCISE WILL MAKE THEM COMFORTABLE.

                    PHIPPS.
: ASIDE. :   D-----D COMFORTABLE.

                    MONT.
: HOLDING UP SWORD C. WITH POINT TO FRONT. :   MESSIEURS!
                            : CAROJAC AND ROUT. CROSS SWORDS :
ALLEZ!
                            : FENCE.   AFTER SOME PASSES, CAROJAC
                            SPRINGS SUDDENLY BACK. :

                    CAROJAC.
: SPRINGING. BACK. :   SACRISTY!

                    ROUT.
: LOWERING HIS SWORD. :   PARDON ME!   I BELIEVE YOU ARE WOUNDED.
                           : THE SECONDS COVER THEIR PRINCIPALS WITH
                           OVERCOATS. :

                    CARO.
: HOLDING HIS LEFT HAND, HIS SWORD BETWEEN HIS TEETH. :   THANK YOU,
M. ROUTLEDGE, FOR THE COURTESY, A MERE SCRATCH.   IT WILL NOT DETAIN
US A MOMENT.   DOCTOR.

: DR. AND MONT. GO TO CAROJAC, ONE SIDE OF
STAGE.   ROUT. JOINS PHIPPS ON THE OTHER
SIDE OF STAGE.   DR. WRAPS BANDAGE ROUND
CAROJAC'S ARM. :

PHIPPS,
: TO ROUT. :   FIRST HIT FOR OUR SIDE! BRAVO!

ROUT,
: SHAKING HIS HEAD. :   MORE LUCK THAN SKILL.   HIS ARM IS MADE OF
STEEL AND WRIST OF INDIA RUBBER.

CARO.
: TO MONT. :   IT WAS HIS AWKWARDNESS, NOT HIS SKILL.   I'LL FINISH
HIM IN TWO PASSES NOW.

PHIPPS,
: TO ROUT. :   ARE YOU COLD?

ROUT.
I'M HOT AS FIRE.

CARO.
: TO MONT. :   FINISSONS!

MONT.
: ALOUD. :   GENTLEMEN!
: THEY FENCE AGAIN.   ENTER STREBELOW,
AS ROUTLEDGE IS DISARMED. :

STREB.
: ON BRIDGE. :   STOP! GENTLEMEN --

: CAROJAC RUNS HIS SWORD THROUGH ROUT. AS
STREB. CRIES STOP. :

ROUT.
: FALLING INTO PHIPPS ARMS. :   TOO LATE!   I KNEW IT.

: ALL TURNING ROUND TO LOOK AT STREBELOW.
MONT. & CAROJAC EXCHANGE LOOKS.   THE
DOCTOR IS PUZZLED. :
MR. STREBELOW!

STREB.

{ COMING FORWARD, C. GOES TO ROUT. }   TOO LATE! IS THERE NO DOCTOR
HERE?

DOCTOR.

{ COMING FORWARD. }   I BEG PARDON, I --
                { GOES TO ROUT. }

STREB,

{ DROPPING ROUT.'S HAND. }   COUNT DE CAROJAC!

CAROJAC.

{ RESUMING HIS COAT }   M. STREBELOW!

STREB.

THE CAUSE OF THIS QUARREL?

PHIPPS.

OF THIS MURDER, STREBELOW?

MONT.

MURDER, SIR!

PHIPPS,

AY, WILFUL, DELIBERATE MURDER.   THE FELLOW FORCED THIS FIGHT, BE-
CAUSE HE KNEW HIS SUPERIOR SKILL.   I CALL IT MURDER.

CARO.

SIR, YOU WILL ANSWER TO ME FOR THIS.

STREB.

{ CALMLY. }   NOT TILL YOU HAVE ANSWERED ME.   THE CAUSE OF THIS
QUARREL?

                { PHIPPS, MONT, CAROJAC LOOK MEANINGLY AT
                EACH OTHER. }

STREB.

WELL, COUNT, ARE YOU ASHAMED TO TELL IT?

                              LILL.
TOO LATE! TOO LATE! OH, HAROLD, HAROLD! MY POOR HAROLD!
                          (THROWS HERSELF BESIDE HIM.)

                              ALL.
MADAME STREBELOW!

                              DOCTOR.
BE CAREFUL, MADAME, YOU MUST NOT STIR HIM.

                              LILL.
OH, HAROLD -- SPEAK! SPEAK TO ME!

                              STREB.
(IN ASTONISHMENT.) MY WIFE!

      .

                              LILL.
DYING -- DYING -- DYING FOR ME, WHO BLIGHTED HIS HEART. HAROLD!
HAROLD! I'VE KILLED HIM -- KILLED HIM!

                              CARO.
(TO STREB. POINTING TO LILL.) WELL, M. STREBELOW, DO YOU UNDER-
STAND THE CAUSE OF THIS QUARREL NOW?

                              STREB.
(RAISING LILL. ASSISTED BY FLORENCE.)   I DO NOT, SIR.

                              CARO.
HE COMPROMISE YOUR WIFE, HE MAKE HER LOVE FOR HIM PUBLIC.
                          (LILL. IS TURNING TO ROUT. HER HANDS EX-
                            TENDED TOWARDS HIM.)

                              STREB.

FAITH AND HER HONOR, I PLEDGE MY LIFE.   AND AGAIN I SAY THIS MAN
LIES, AND FOR THIS LIE, I WILL HOLD HIM ACCOUNTABLE AT THE PROPER
TIME AND IN THE PROPER PLACE.

C U R T A I N.

A C T I V.

---oOo---

S C E N E 2 N D.   B O U D O I R.
                          ┆ AT RISE OF CURTAIN ENTER LIZETTE L.C.
                          FOLLOWED BY STREBELOW, LILLIAN ON HIS
                          ARM, THEN MRS. BROWN.   STREBELOW HALF
                          LEADS, HALF SUPPORTS LILLIAN TO SOFA,
                          R.C. ON WHICH SHE SINKS EXHAUSTED. ┆

                          STREB.
┆ TO FLORENCE. ┆ BELIEVE ME, I AM VERY GRATEFUL FOR YOUR KIND AT-
TENTION TO LILLIAN; SHE SEEMS BETTER NOW, ┆ CROSSING TO LIZETTE. ┆
LET THE CARRIAGE WAIT.
                          ┆ EXIT LIZETTE. ┆

                          FLOR.
┆ APPROACHING LILL. ┆ ALL SHE NEEDS IS A LITTLE REST -- A LITTLE
SLEEP. ┆ TO LILL. ┆ YOU DO FEEL BETTER NOW?

                          LILL.
YES -- YES -- MUCH BETTER, THANK YOU.   IT WAS THE SHOCK -- THE
SHOCK -- IS HAROLD -- IS MR. ROUTLEDGE DEAD?

                          STREB,
I TRUST NOT!

                          LILL.
FOR HEAVEN'S SAKE SEND AND SEE!

                          FLOR.
DR. WATSON PROMISED TO COME HERE AS SOON AS HE ASCERTAINED THAT MR.
ROUTLEDGE HAD BEEN SAFELY MOVED.

                          LILL.
THE SUSPENSE WILL KILL ME!
                          ┆ RISES AND WALKS, CROSSES TO L.H. BACK
                          TO R. C. ┆

10

<u>: DURING THIS SCENE UP TO THE ENTRANCE OF
DOCTOR, STREBELOW IS INTENTLY WATCHING
LILLIAN.:</u>

MRS. BROWN.

: <u>FOLLOWS HER.</u> :   DO CALM YOURSELF, LILLIAN! DO NOT LOOK SO WILD.
YOU FRIGHTEN ME.   I'M SURE WE ALL SHARE YOUR HORROR.

<u>LILL.</u>

BUT WHO CAN **SHARE** MY FEELINGS?   DID YOU SEE THE LOOK OF REPROACH-
FUL ANGUISH HIS EYES CAST UPON ME ERE THEY CLOSED -- CLOSED, PER-
HAPS FOR EVER?   I SHALL GO MAD! MAD!

<u>STREB.</u>

: <u>ASIDE. CROSSES BACK TO L.</u> : ''REPROACHFUL ANGUISH.''   : <u>ALOUD.</u> :
I WILL SEND -- THERE, THERE DEAR!   : <u>RINGS BELL ON TABLE, L.H.</u> :
SWORD THRUSTS ARE NOT ALWAYS FATAL.   SIT DOWN, COMPOSE YOURSELF.
: <u>ENTER LIZETTE.   SITS AT L.H. TABLE AND WRITES.</u> :   SEND TO THIS
ADDRESS, AND INQUIRE AS TO THE CONDITION OF MR. ROUTLEDGE,   LET
THE MESSENGER TAKE THE CARRIAGE AND RETURN AT ONCE.   : <u>EXIT LIZ.</u> :
: TO MRS. BROWN.| YOU MUST NOT BE SURPRISED AT THE EXTREME AGITA-
TION OF LILLIAN, HAROLD ROUTLEDGE AND SHE WERE OLD PLAYMATES, AND
THE SENSIBILITY OF --

MRS. BROWN.

: C : MY DEAR MR. STREBELOW, I'M FAIRLY ASTONISHED AT BEING ALIVE
MYSELF.   THE SNOW, THE MOONLIGHT, THE GREY RUINS OF THE HISTORIC
CHATEAU, THE SUDDENNESS OF THE STRIFE, THE ROMANTIC ARISTOCRACY,
AND THE ARISTOCRATIC ROMANCE OF THE AFFAIR MADE IT ALL LIKE A NOVEL
TILL I SAW HAROLD ROUTLEDGE'S BLOOD ON THAT MAN'S SWORD,   : <u>LILL</u>
<u>STARTS UP FROM SOFA, CROSSES TO R.H.</u> :   OH! OH! THEN I FELT AS
BADLY, AS HORRIFIED AS LILLIAN HERSELF.   BUT : TO LILL.: DO
CALM YOURSELF, DEAR.

<u>LILL.</u>

YES, YES -- WHEN THE NEWS COMES, I'LL BE CALM -- CALM!

MRS. BROWN.

I ALWAYS LIKED ROUTLEDGE.   THERE WAS NONE OF THE PLEBEAN ABOUT
HIM.   I RECOLLECT HOW GLAD I WAS WHEN IT WAS REPORTED THAT YOU AND
HE WERE ENGAGED.

STREB.

ENGAGED! ENGAGED TO WHAT?

LILL.

[STOPPING SHORT, HER BACK TO AUDIENCE AND TO STREB.]   ENGAGED TO
BE MARRIED.

MRS. BROWN.

WHY, STREBELOW, YOU DON'T MEAN TO SAY THAT YOU DID NOT KNOW LILLIAN
WESTBROOK AND HAROLD ROUTLEDGE WERE ONCE CONSIDERED THE LUCIA AND
EDGARDO OF NEW YORK SOCIETY? WHY, THE MATCH WAS --

LILL.

[HER BACK TO AUDIENCE.]   PLEASE SAY NO MORE -- ABOUT -- THE --
                            [TURNS ROUND, LOOKS AT STREBELOW, AT MRS.
                            BROWN.   TOTTERS -- STREB. RUNS AND CATCH-
                            ES HER IN HIS ARMS AS SHE IS ABOUT TO
                            FALL.   CROSSES AND PLACES HER ON SOFA
                            R. C.]

STREB.

TAKE COURAGE -- TAKE COURAGE -- I'M SURE YOUR OLD FRIEND IS SAFE.
IT IS ALL RIGHT! ALL RIGHT!

LILL.

[LOOKING AT STREB. PITEOUSLY.]   IT NEVER WAS RIGHT.

                            [AS STREBELOW IS BENDING OVER LILLIAN
                            HIS BACK TO THE DOOR, ENTER DR. WATSON
                            SEEN ONLY BY MRS. BROWN.   SHE GOES TO
                            HIM QUICKLY, CATCHES HIM BY THE WRIST.]

MRS. BROWN.

IS HE DEAD?

DOCTOR.

[TO MRS. BROWN.]   NO, BUT HE CANNOT LIVE AN HOUR.

MRS. BROWN.

IF YOU SAY THAT HERE, YOU'LL KILL MRS. STREBELOW.   BE CAREFUL!
[ALOUD.]   HERE IS THE DOCTOR.

LILL.

: SPRINGING TO HER FEET. :   AT LAST! AT LAST! : GOES TOWARDS DR. :
TELL ME THE TRUTH -- THE TRUTH.   IS HAROLD ROUTLEDGE DEAD?

DOCTOR.

NO -- NO! HE IS BADLY WOUNDED, BUT NOT DEAD.

LILL.

IS THERE ANY HOPE?

DOCTOR.

WHILE THERE'S LIFE, SCIENCE SEES HOPE.

STREB.

: ENCOURAGINGLY. :   THERE, THERE! I TOLD YOU SO.
: PASSING HER OVER TO SOFA. :

LILL.

THANK HEAVEN!
: SINKS ON SOFA.   STREB GOES OVER TO R.C. :

MRS. BROWN.

: BEHIND SOFA. :   NOW DEAR, YOU MUST REST.   THE DOCTOR WILL TAKE
ME HOME.   I'M SURE POOR BROWN MUST BE IN A DREADFUL STATE.   I'LL
CALL EARLY TO-MORROW.   NOW GO, AND BE SURE YOU TAKE A GOOD SLEEP.
GOOD-BYE! GOOD-BYE! DON'T RISE.

STREB.

: CROSSING TO C. :   GOOD-BYE, AND THANK YOU.

DOCTOR.

GOOD-BYE, MR. STREBELOW, AND IF THERE IS ANY CHANGE FOR EITHER THE
WORSE OR THE BETTER, I WILL COME AND LET YOU KNOW.   I'M GOING TO
HIM AS SOON AS I HAVE LEFT MRS. BROWN AT HOME.

LILL.

DO, DO!

STREB.

GOOD-BYE.
: EXIT MRS. BROWN AND DR. L.3.E.
STREBELOW AND LILLIAN,   SOLUS. :

STREB.

WELL, LILLIAN, YOU HAD BEST RETIRE.

LILL.

'TIS NO USE, JOHN, I COULD NOT SLEEP.

STREB.

WILL YOU GO TO NATALIE?

LILL.

NOT YET.   BEFORE I GO TO HER -- I MUST --

STREB.

: WITH FORCED CALMNESS. :   SPEAK TO ME?   BETTER POSTPONE IT TILL
TO-MORROW.   YOU ARE EXHAUSTED.   I CAN WAIT.

LILL.

NO, EVERY MOMENT OF DOUBT, OF ANXIETY WOULD BUT EXHAUST ME MORE.
I WILL HEAR YOU NOW.

STREB.

HEAR ME?   I THOUGHT IT WAS YOU WHO WISHED TO SPEAK --

LILL.

IT IS! IT IS! BUT I FEAR TO BEGIN.

STREB.

LET ME HELP YOU.   YOU LOVE HAROLD ROUTLEDGE, DO YOU NOT?

LILL.

I DO NOT KNOW.   I DID LOVE HIM.

STREB.

AND WERE ENGAGED TO HIM?

LILL.

: SURPRISED. :   YES, CERTAINLY, I WAS.

STREB.

AND HE LOVED YOU?

LILL.

WHAT BROKE THE ENGAGEMENT?

LILL,

A LOVER'S QUARREL.

STREB,

AND YOU HAVE LOVED HIM EVER SINCE?

LILL.

I DO NOT KNOW.

STREB.

YOU DO NOT KNOW? YET EXCEPT MYSELF, EVERYBODY SEEMED TO KNOW IT.
THE PAINTER SAW IT ON YOUR FACE AND PLACED IT ON HIS CANVAS, THE
SHALLOW CRITIC READ IT AND DECLARED IT. AND I -- I -- YOUR HUSBAND
LIVING BY YOUR SIDE EVERY DAY, EVERY HOUR FOR SIX YEARS -- I -- I
DID NOT SEE IT, DID NOT FEEL IT! : BITTERLY.: LOVE IS BLIND,
INDEED! OH, FOOL! FOOL!

LILL,

BUT JOHN, YOU KNEW --

STREB.

I KNEW! KNEW WHAT? WHAT I KNOW NOW, WHAT IT HAS TAKEN ME SIX
YEARS TO KNOW IS THAT THE HEART ON WHICH I REPOSED, IN WHICH I
SHRINED A MAN'S TRUEST LOVE HAS BEEN VEILED TO ME AS A SANCTUARY
TO WHOSE RELIGION I WAS A STRANGER.   YET I WORSHIPPED AT IT WITH
THE DEVOTION OF A SAINT, TRUSTED IT WITH MY MAN'S FAITH, MY ALL.--

LILL.

: DRAWING HERSELF UP IN PRIDE.:   NOR HAS THE TRUST BEEN BETRAYED.
MY DUTY AND YOUR HONOR --

STREB,

DUTY! HONOR! WHO SPOKE OF HONOR?   I SPOKE AND SPEAK OF LOVE, OF
THAT LOVE WHICH IN A WIFE IS THE SOLE INVULNERABLE ARMOR OF A HUS-
BAND'S HONOR -- OF THAT LOVE WITHOUT WHICH HONOR IS VALUELESS, AND
LIFE A BLANK -- OF THE LOVE IN WHICH HONOR DWELLS AS UNCONSCIOUSLY
AS FLOWERS BLOOM AND WATER FLOWS.   GOD HELP THE HUSBAND WHOSE
HONOR IS GUARDED BY DUTY ALONE.

STREB,

BEFORE! BEFORE WHAT?

LILL,

BEFORE WE WERE MARRIED,

STREB,

BELIEVING THAT WITH YOUR HAND I RECEIVED YOUR HEART, WHY SHOULD I
HAVE SAID IT?

LILL,

YOU KNEW I HAD BEEN ENGAGED TO HAROLD ROUTLEDGE, THAT BUT A FEW
DAYS BEFORE YOU PROPOSED TO MY FATHER FOR ME, IT WAS SETTLED I WAS
TO BE HIS WIFE.

STREB,

(SURPRISED,) HOW SHOULD I KNOW IT? YOU NEVER MENTIONED HIM TO
ME.

LILL,

BUT MY FATHER TOLD YOU?

STREB,

NEVER! NEVER!

LILL,

THEN MY FATHER DECEIVED ME.

STREB,

BUT WHY, WHY?

LILL,

THAT I CANNOT TELL, UNLESS IT WAS TO --

STREB,

TO WHAT?

LILL,

UNLESS IT WAS TO AVOID ANY DELAY OF OUR MARRIAGE. IMMEDIATE RUIN--

STREB,

IMMEDIATE RUIN! THEN YOU KNEW OF THE THREATENING BANKRUPTCY?

LILL.

[ASTONISHED.]   CERTAINLY.

STREB.

[STAGGERED.]   AND -- AND -- ACCEPTED ME TO AVERT IT?

LILL.

TO SAVE MY FATHER -- YES.

STREB.

THEN YOUR FATHER DECEIVED ME -- DECEIVED US BOTH!

LILLIAN.

[FRIGHTENED.]   OH FATHER!
                  [SITS R.C. ON SOFA.]

STREB.

THEN I DID NOT MARRY YOU, I BOUGHT YOU.   I BECAME, NOT YOUR HUS-
BAND, BUT YOUR OWNER.   THIS MARRIAGE WAS NOT A UNION, BUT A SAC-
RIFICE.   A SACRIFICE, NOT OF ONE, NOT OF TWO, BUT OF THREE LIVES.
OH, HEAVEN!   WHAT HAVE WE DONE?   I SEE IT ALL -- I SEE IT ALL!
                  [FALLS INTO CHAIR, L.H.]

LILL.

[RISES, GOES TO STREB.]   CAN YOU FORGIVE ME?

STREB.

[HIS FACE IN HIS HANDS.]   WAIT!   WAIT!

                  [PAUSE.   LILLIAN IS KNEELING BY STREB-
                  ELOW'S KNEE.   BOTH ARE WEEPING.]

STREB.

WE MUST NOT FORGET OUR CHILD.

LILL.

[RAISES HER HEAD.]   NATALIE!

STREB.

STREB.

I HAVE NOTHING TO FORGIVE, BUT MY BLINDNESS.   I SHOULD HAVE THOUGHT
FOR BOTH.   I WILL DO SO NOW.   TELL ME, AND TELL ME FRANKLY, FOR
FRANKNESS NOW ALONE CAN SAVE US, DO YOU STILL LOVE HAROLD ROUTLEDGE?

LILL.

I DON'T KNOW.

: RISING, CROSSING TO R.C. :

STREB.

: RISING AND FOLLOWING HER. :   DO YOU NOT KNOW YOUR OWN HEART?
DON'T SOB SO, BE CALM.

LILL.

I DID LOVE HAROLD ROUTLEDGE, I BELIEVE, WITH THE LOVE OF A SCHOOL-
GIRL.

STREB.

WELL, WELL?

LILL.

WE HAD A SILLY QUARREL -- BROKE OUR ENGAGEMENT.

STREB.

GO ON -- GO ON!

LILL.

I WROTE HIM TO COME BACK TO ME THE VERY DAY I ACCEPTED YOU.   HE
CAME BACK, DOUBTLESS FULL OF JOY OF HOPE OF LOVE -- FOR HE DID LOVE
ME.

: SOBS. :

STREB.

: THOUGHTFULLY. :   I RECOLLECT.

LILL.

: PITEOUSLY. :   I REFUSED TO SEE HIM, WHAT COULD I DO?

STREB.

WELL, AFTER THAT?

                         STREB.
I UNDERSTAND.

                         LILL.
I COULD NOT UNDERSTAND, I NEVER DID! YOUR KIND LOVE, YOUR WATCH-
FULNESS, YOUR DEVOTION WON UPON MY MOTHER'S HEART.

                         STREB.
YES -- YES.

                         LILL.
BUT I FEARED TO SHOW IT. I SCARCELY UNDERSTOOD MY OWN FEELINGS, --
TILL -- TILL HE RETURNED. BUT WHEN I SAW HIM, WHOSE LIFE I KNEW
I HAD BLIGHTED, LYING THERE DYING, AS I FEARED, REMORSE -- SHAME
TOOK POSSESSION OF ME -- POSSESS ME STILL. I -- I --
                   [SITS R; C. ON SOFA.]

                         STREB.
SPOKE AND ACTED LIKE THE NOBLE WOMAN THAT YOU ARE.

                         LILL.
AND YOU DO FORGIVE ME?

                         STREB.
AGAIN I SAY THERE IS NOTHING TO FORGIVE, BUT MY BLINDNESS, AND YOUR
FATHER'S FOLLY.

                         LILL.
AND YOU WILL FORGET IT ALL?

                         STREB.
AND CONTINUE OUR MUTUAL SACRIFICE? THAT WERE TO PUNISH YOU. NO, NO!

                         LILL.
WHAT WILL YOU DO?

                         STREB.
LEAVE YOU -- FOR A TIME, MAYBE. NATALIE -- POOR CHILD OF A LOVE-
LESS UNION.

19

STREB.

: BITTERLY, ASIDE.:   OH, HOW LITTLE SHE KNOWS ME, YET.   : ALOUD.:
NO, POOR MOTHER, YOU SHALL KEEP YOUR CHILD.   I WOULD REMAIN WITH
YOU, TOO, WERE I A STRONGER MAN THAN I AM.   I CAN READ CLEARLY
WHAT IS PASSING IN YOUR HEART, BUT AFTER SEEING YOU SACRIFICE IT
TO YOUR FATHER, I WILL NOT WEAKLY TEMPT YOU TO SACRIFICE IT AGAIN
TO YOUR CHILD.

LILL.

: PITEOUSLY.:   AND YOU WILL LEAVE ME?

STREB.

WITH YOUR FATHER?

LILL.

AND WHEN WILL YOU RETURN?

STREB.

WHEN YOUR HEART CALLS ME, WHEN IT CALLS THE HUSBAND AS WELL AS THE
FATHER.

LILL.

REMAIN WITH ME, AND TRUST ME.

STREB.

NEAR OR FAR, 'TIS NOT YOU I FEAR TO TRUST, 'TIS MYSELF.   TO LIVE
BESIDE YOU, DAY BY DAY, TO HEAR YOU EVERY HOUR, CONSTRUING EACH
HEAVE OF YOUR BOSOM INTO A SIGH FOR ANOTHER, EACH MOMENT OF AB-
STRACTION INTO A DREAM OF HIM!   NO -- NO!   I'M NOT STRONG ENOUGH
FOR THAT.

LILL.

THEN BE IT AS YOU WILL.

STREB.

IT MUST BE SO.   GO TO NATALIE.
                              : LILL. GOES TO R.   PAUSES, EXITS R.I.E.:

STREB.

: SOLUS.:   'TIS ALL OVER!   : WALKS UP AND DOWN STAGE.:   STOPS
BEFORE THE PICTURE.:   HOW PLAIN ITS STORY SEEMS NOW!   THAT FACE,
SO LONG TO ME THE SUM OF EARTHLY BEAUTY, THE OBJECT OF ALL MY PRIDE

20

IN THE PAST, THE PREFIGURATION OF ALL MY HOPES IN THE FUTURE,—— NOW
TELLS ME ONLY OF THE SUFFERING VICTIM CARRYING IN HER HEART A SE-
CRET THAT MUST NOT LIVE   : IN AGONY.:   A LOVE THAT CANNOT DIE!
                           : PAUSE, WHILE STREB. LOOKS AT PICTURE
                           IN SILENCE.:

                    LIZETTE.

A LETTER, SIR.

                    : STREBELOW STILL LOOKING AT PICTURE.
                    LIZETTE PLACES LETTER IN HIS HAND, WHICH
                    RESTS ON HIS KNEE.   EXIT LIZETTE.L.3.E:

                    STREB.

I WILL LOOK AT IT NO MORE.   LET THE FACE BE VEILED TO ME IN THE
FUTURE, AS THE HEART HAS BEEN IN THE PAST.   : DRAWS CURTAIN OVER
PICTURE. AS HE DOES SO DROPS LETTER. PICKS IT UP, WALKS DOWN
STAGE, OPENS LETTER. :   ROUTLEDGE DEAD! DEAD! LEAVING HER A WIDOW
WITH A LIVING HUSBAND, AND LEAVING ME A WIFELESS HUSBAND AND A
CHILDLESS FATHER.

                    : DROPS INTO CHAIR.:

                    C U R T A I N.

<u>A C T   5.</u>

---0-0-0---

<u>BABBAGE.</u>
THE PAPERS ARE ALL RIGHT, OLD BOY.   THIS ONE IS MINE-- AND THAT
ONE, YOURS.   :AS HE SPEAKS BABBAGE SPREADS TWO WRITTEN SHEETS OF
LEGAL CAP ON TABLE-- PUSHING PEN TOWARDS WESTBROOK WHO TAKES IT
AND SIGNS EACH-- THROWS DOWN PEN AND TURNS AWAY.:   IS THAT ALL
THE FUSS YOU MAKE ABOUT IT, OLD FELLOW?   IT TAKES BUT A SINGLE
CLIP TO CUT THE LONGEST CHAIN.   :WIPES HIS EYES.:

<u>WEST.</u>
:IN EVIDENT EMOTION, RISES-- SHAKES HANDS WITH BABBAGE.:   STAUNCH
FRIEND AND PARTNER OF THIRTY YEARS---- I--- I--

<u>BABBAGE.</u>
THAT'S ALL RIGHT-- WESTBROOK-- ALL RIGHT-- DON'T MIND ME-- I'M A
STUPID OLD FOOL I SUPPOSE.   HERE GOES!
                              :SIGNS THE PAPER IN TURN.   HANDS ONE TO
                              WESTBROOK, PUTTING THE OTHER IN HIS POCKET:

<u>WEST.</u>
AND NOW---

<u>BABBAGE.</u>
AND NOW THE LAST PAPERS ARE SIGNED THAT DISSOLVE THE FIRM OF BAB-
BAGE AND WESTBROOK, AFTER AN EXISTENCE OF TWENTY NINE YEARS, ELEVEN
MONTHS AND FIFTEEN DAYS.   WELL, ARE YOU SATISFIED?   WE RETIRE
WITH A LITTLE OVER TWO MILLIONS AND A HALF APIECE-- OWING NO MAN
A DOLLAR.

<u>WEST.</u>
IF FIGURES NEVER LIE, WE ARE TWO HIGHLY SUCCESSFUL MEN.

BABBAGE,

BOTH OUR SHARES SECURELY INVESTED. GOVERNMENT BONDS-- REAL ES-
TATE-- A. NUMBER ONE-- TWO COPPER FASTENED IRON BOUND, SOLID BUS-
INESS MEN. IS THAT SUCCESS?

WEST,

IF FIGURES NEVER LIE.

BABBAGE,

HM! FIGURES ARE THE BIGGEST LIARS IN THE WORLD. GIVE A BOY A
ONE DOLLAR BILL AND TELL HIM TO MULTIPLY THE AMOUNT OF HAPPINESS
HE CAN GET OUT OF IT BY TWO MILLIONS, FIVE HUNDRED THOUSAND-- HE
WILL HARDLY BELIEVE THAT YOU AND I ENVY HIM THE HAPPINESS HE EX-
TRACTS FROM THE FIRST TEN CENTS HE SPENDS-- KNOWING HE HAS ENOUGH
LEFT FOR THE CIRCUS AND ALL THE SIDE SHOWS. HEIGH HO! WESTBROOK,
THE BIGGER THE FIGURES, THE BIGGER THEY LIE.

WEST,

:SIGHING.: RATHER LATE TO TAKE THAT VIEW OF THEM NOW.

BABB,

:RISING.: HM! WESTBROOK, THERE IS ONE MORE DOCUMENT-- I... I...
:ASIDE.: SOME PEOPLE WOULD CALL ME AN OLD FOOL, I SUPPOSE-- IF
THEY KNEW IT! :ALOUD.: THERE IS ONE MORE DOCUMENT I WANT TO
TRANSFER-- IT ISN'T A VERY SHARP FINANCIAL OPERATION, :TAKES
PEPER OUT OF HIS POCKET, HANDS IT TO WESTBROOK.: BUT IT WILL EASE
MY CONSCIENCE A LITTLE.

WEST,

:READING OUTSIDE OF PAPER.: A WARRANTEE DEED-- TO LILLIAN WEST-
BROOK STREBELON! :OPENS PAPER, GLANCES OVER IT.: GRAND STREET
PROPERTY! MY DEAR BABBAGE, WHAT DO YOU MEAN? THIS PROPERTY IS
WORTH OVER HALF A MILLION. WE ALLOWED THAT MUCH FOR IT IN THE
DIVISION OF OUR ASSETS.

BABB,

IT'S ONLY THE ODD HALF MILLION, OLD BOY. YOU AND I OWN FIVE
MILLIONS OF DOLLARS BETWEEN US-- TAKE IT LARRY-- FORGIVE ME FOR
BRINGING IT UP, BUT... BUT IT'S BEEN ON MY CONSCIENCE FOR THE
LAST NINE YEARS. BY RIGHTS, WE OWE IT ALL TO LILLIAN-- POOR GIRL!
I KNOW IT ISN'T MONEY SHE NEEDS-- SHE HAS ENOUGH OF THAT-- BUT AN
OLD BRUTE LIKE ME HAS NOTHING BUT MONEY TO GIVE HER. IT WON'T
HELP HER ANY, I KNOW-- BUT IT MAY HELP TO EASE MY CONSCIENCE A
LITTLE. IT'S ONLY THE ODD HALF MILLION, LARRY.

                          WEST,
⌞MUCH AFFECTED.⌟   AH, OLD FRIEND AND WISE PARTNER, YOU SAW BETTER
THAN I ...

                          BABB,
THERE, THERE, OLD FELLOW-- FORGIVE ME FROM BRINGING IT UP--   BUT
HOW IS SHE, TO-DAY?

                          WEST,
JUST AS SHE WAS YESTERDAY-- AS SHE WAS LAST WEEK-- LAST MONTH--
LAST YEAR-- AS SHE HAS BEEN EVERY DAY SINCE JOHN STREBELON GAVE
HER BACK TO ME IN PARIS WITH THE WORDS, ''TAKE BACK YOUR DAUGHTER,
MR. WESTBROOK, AND BE IT YOUR TASK TO SOFTEN TO HER THE MEMORIES
OF THE PAST YOU MADE FOR HER AND ME.'' YOU KNOW HOW I BROUGHT HER
HOME-- HOW JOHN STREBELON MADE HER PRACTICALLY MISTRESS OF THE
BULK OF HIS FORTUNE, NOW SETTLED ON THEIR CHILD, HOW SINCE THEN
HE HAS RESIDED IN ROME.   I DO NOT BELIEVE HE EVER RETURNED TO
PARIS AFTER HIS TERRIBLE DUEL WITH THE COUNT DE CAROJAC.

                          BABB,
AND HE NEVER WRITES TO YOU?

                          WEST,
NEVER... BUT I BELIEVE HE CORRESPONDS REGULARLY WITH FANNY HOLCOMB.
OH, BABBAGE, BABBAGE-- HAD I BUT HEEDED YOUR WARNING ON THAT DREAD-
FUL DAY!

                          BABB,
WE SHOULD NOT BE SHARING FIVE MILLIONS TO-DAY-- BUT I SHOULD FEEL
A HAPPIER AND A BETTER MAN.

                          WEST,
I'D GIVE EVERY PENNY OF IT TO BRING HAROLD ROUTLEDGE BACK TO LIFE--
TO COMPENSATE TO JOHN STREBELON.

                          BABB,
THE LATTER AT ALL EVENTS IS POSSIBLE.

                          WEST,
HOW?

                          BABB,
LISTEN.   JUST AS SURE AS JOHN STREBELON LOVES YOUR DAUGHTER-- JUST

AS SURE-- YOUR DAUGHTER NOW LOVES HIM AND HUNGERS FOR HIM, TO-DAY,

WEST,

WOULD TO HEAVEN IT WERE TRUE,

BABBAGE,

IT IS TRUE, SINCE WE COMMENCED WINDING UP OUR BUSINESS, I HAVE BEEN HERE EVERY DAY, I HAVE REPEATEDLY SEEN LILLIAN AND NATALIE TOGETHER-- I NEVER HEARD THEM TALK OF NATALIE'S FATHER-- THAT LIL-LIAN DID NOT TELL THE CHILD HOW GREAT AND GOOD HER FATHER IS, NATALIE WRITES TO HIM REGULARLY; AND LILLIAN OVERSEES THE COR-RESPONDENCE,

WEST,

[EAGERLY,] HOW DO YOU KNOW THIS?

BABB,

ABOUT A MONTH AGO-- THE DAY THAT ILLINOIS CENTRAL BOUNDED UP TO NINETY-TWO AND TUMBLED BACK TO EIGHTY-SEVEN-- NATALIE CAME TO ME WITH A CURIOUS LITTLE LETTER IN HER HAND-- THE DAY PERKINS AND JOHNSON WENT UNDER, YOU KNOW-- SHORT ON ERIE AND WABASH-- PACIFIC MAIL WENT CLEAN OUT OF SIGHT, NATALIE ASKED ME TO PUT A LITTLE PICTURE, AS SHE CALLED A STAMP, ON HER LETTER AND DROP IT INTO THE BOX THAT GOES TO ROME, THE LETTER WAS ADDRESSED TO JOHN STREB-ELON, IT IS EXACTLY FIVE WEEKS AGO, TAKE MY WORD FOR IT, LIL-LIAN IS TRYING TO WOO HER HUSBAND-- AND THE CHILD IS WRITING THE LOVE LETTER,

WEST,

HEAVEN GRANT IT-- BUT BABBAGE-- [HOLDING OUT PAPER,]

DADD,

WELL?

WEST,

THIS GIFT-- REALLY I CANNOT--

BABB,

LET ME HAVE MY OWN WAY ABOUT THAT, OLD BOY, IT IS A PRIVATE SPEC-ULATION OF MY OWN, [OPENS DOOR R, I, E, GOING TOWARDS DOOR,] IT'S ONLY THE ODD HALF MILLION, [REACHES DOOR, TURNS ROUND,] HERE COMES ANOTHER WHO HAS RETIRED FROM BUSINESS TOO-- ONLY TO

SECURE AN ACTIVE PARTNERSHIP PRETTY SOON, :LAUGHING.: I THINK.

                    WEST.
WHO IS IT?

                    BABB.
:LAUGHING.:   THE RELICT OF THE LATE MR. BROWN.   I HEAR HER IN
THE HALL.

                    WEST.
:GOING.:   THEN COME THIS WAY, :TO UPPER DOOR.: TO MY ROOM.
:WESTBROOK LEADS OFF BY UPPER DOOR-- BABBAGE TURNS TO FOLLOW THAT
WAY, GOING LAST-- TALKING AS HE GOES.:

                    BABB.
BUT I'VE KEPT THE OTHER TWO MILLION-- WHAT A HEARTLESS GRASPING
SET WE SOLID BUSINESS MEN ARE.
                    :EXITS UPPER DOOR FOLLOWING WEST.:

                    :ENTER FLORENCE, LOWER DOOR.:

                    FLORENCE.
MR. BABBAGE!   :CROSSING TO L. H.:

                    BABB.
:TURNING BACK.:   MRS. BROWN!

                    FLORENCE.
HOW IS LILLIAN, TO-DAY?   :RINGS BELL.:

                    BABB.
:AT DOOR.:   THE DOCTOR WAS HERE HALF AN HOUR AGO.

                    FLOR.
WHAT DID HE SAY?

                    BABB.
:COMING INTO ROOM.:   NOTHING.

                    FLOR.
PSHA!   IF I WERE NOT A WOMAN I COULD SAY THAT MYSELF.   :ENTER

6

LIZETTE L. D.: EXCUSE ME ONE MOMENT, MR. BABBAGE. [TO SERVANT.] TELL MRS. HOLCOMB, I WILL RUN UP TO SEE HER. I WANT TO SEE HER ON BUSINESS.

BABB.

BUSINESS!

[EXIT LIZETTE.]

FLOR.

[TO BABBAGE WHO COMES DOWN STAGE.] I WAS ON MY WAY DOWN TOWN TO ORDER SOME NEW CARDS. [TAKES OUT A CARD WITH A WIDE BLACK MARGIN] I CAME IN TO ASK AUNT FANNY HOW WIDE I OUGHT NOW TO HAVE THE MAR-GIN.

BABB.

YOU CALL THAT BUSINESS?

FLOR.

CERTAINLY. AUNT FANNY IS A WIDOW, LIKE MYSELF-- WHAT DO YOU THINK, MR. BABBAGE? [HANDS BABB. CARD. HE TAKES IT GRAVELY, LOOKS AT IT THROUGH HIS SPECTACLES.] THE TWO YEARS ARE UP TO-MORROW.

BABB.

WESTBROOK AND I BOUGHT AND SOLD STOCK FOR MR. BROWN FOR UPWARDS OF TWENTY YEARS-- BROWN ALWAYS LIKED A PRETTY WIDE MARGIN HIMSELF. [HANDS CARD BACK TO FLOR.] ALWAYS ALLOWED A WIDE MARGIN TOO-- ONE GOOD MARGIN DESERVES ANOTHER.

FLOR.

[L. H.] POOR DEAR OLD BROWN! [RUNNING HER FINGERS ROUND THE CARD.] I'LL KEEP IT WIDE. HEIGH HO! HOW DO YOU LIKE MY NEW DRESS, MR. BABBAGE? NEAT, ISN'T IT? MADAME RAYPANGSAY IS SO VERY ARTISTIC! IT IS A VERY DELICATE MATTER FOR A DRESSMAKER TO GUIDE A YOUNG WIDOW THROUGH THE VARIOUS STAGES OF HER AFFLICTION WITH GOOD TASTE:-- ABSOLUTE WRETCHEDNESS-- DEEP GRIEF-- PROFOUND MELANCHOLY-- CHRISTIAN RESIGNATION-- SENTIMENTAL SADNESS.

BABB.

I TRUST YOUR PHYSICIAN HAS HOPES OF YET PULLING YOU THROUGH.

7

FLOR.

THE IMMEDIATE DANGER IS PAST. FIRST: HE PRESCRIBED RETIREMENT
FROM THE WORLD. SEVERE AS IT WAS, I TOOK THE DOSE. SECOND: HE
PRESCRIBED CHANGE OF AIR.

BABB.

YOU TOOK THE DOSE-- AT SARATOGA?

FLOR.

NO-- SARATOGA WAS TOO GAY-- HEIGH HO! I RETIRED TO NEWPORT!
I AM NOW A PROMISING CONVALESCENT. THE DOCTOR TOLD ME HE HAD BUT
ONE MORE PRESCRIPTION TO SUGGEST. REALLY, -- I --

BABB.

:DRILY.: A SECOND HUSBAND.

FLOR.

YES.

BABB.

WILL YOU TAKE IT?

FLOR.

:LAUGHING.: WITH ALL MY HEART!

BABB.

YOU HAVE SOMETHING MORE SUBSTANTIAL THAN THAT TO OFFER YOUR SECOND
HUSBAND.

FLOR.

THANKS TO MY FIRST, I HAVE. HEIGH HO! :CROSSES TO R.: DON'T
YOU THINK THERE IS DELICATE SUGGESTION OF SUBDUED GRIEF IN THIS
KNIFE PLEATING, MR. BABBAGE?
                              :WITHOUT WAITING FOR AN ANSWER FLOR.,
                              LOOKING AT HER DRESS, GOES TO LOWER DOOR,
                              LOOKS AT HER TRAIN OVER HER SHOULDER, AT
                              DOOR, KISSES HER HAND TO BABBAGE AND
                              EXITS.:

BABB.

:LOOKING AFTER HER A MOMENT.: POOR BROWN! ALWAYS SO ANXIOUS
ABOUT HIS MARGIN! THERE IS NOTHING BUT A MARGIN LEFT OF HIM NOW!

8

BROWN WAS ONE OF US-- A SOLID BUSINESS MAN!

{GOES TO UPPER DOOR AS HE TALKS, EXITS
SHAKING HIS HEAD.}

FANNY.

{OUTSIDE, UPPER DOOR AS IF MEETING BABBAGE IN THE HALL.}   AH, MR.
BABBAGE, -- MR. WESTBROOK IS UP STAIRS--

BABB.

YES-- I KNOW.

{ENTER FANNY R. U. E. CROSSES TO L.}

FANNY.

{LOOKING ROUND.}   NOT HERE.

LILL.

{ENTERING UPPER DOOR.}   LOOKING FOR ME, AUNT?   I HEARD YOU COME
DOWN STAIRS.

FANNY.

{SITTING DOWN L. C.}   YES, DEAR.   SIT DOWN.   {LILLIAN GETS STOOL,
SITS BY FANNY.}   HAVE YOU THOUGHT OF WHAT I HAVE SAID TO YOU?

LILL.

I HAVE NEVER CEASED TO THINK OF IT.

FANNY.

YOU ARE GROWING MORE AND MORE LISTLESS.   YOUR HEALTH MUST GIVE WAY
AT LAST---

LILL.

{DEJECTEDLY.}   I AM SO WRETCHED-- SO MISERABLE-- HAVE BEEN ALL
THESE YEARS.

FANNY.

I KNEW IT ALL THE TIME.   WHY DO YOU NOT WRITE TO HIM?

LILL.

I DARE NOT?

FANNY.

{COAXINGLY.}   WHY, DEAR?

9

LILL.

OH, AUNT-- IF YOU HAD SEEN, HAD HEARD HIM THAT TERRIBLE NIGHT,
WHEN HE IN HIS ANGER AND DISAPPOINTMENT REVEALED TO ME THE DEPTH
OF HIS AFFECTION-- THE NOBILITY OF HIS MANLY NATURE-- REVEALED TO
ME WHAT I WOULD NOT CONFESS TO MYSELF, THAT I DID LOVE HIM, HAD
LONG LOVED HIM, WHOM I BELIEVED ME WITHOUT A SINGLE THOUGHT OF
LOVE-- IF YOU HAD SEEN THAT-- HEARD THAT, YOU WOULD UNDERSTAND WHY
I DARE NOT WRITE TO HIM NOW.

FANNY.

COULD HE SEE WHAT I HAVE SEEN, HEARD WHAT I HAVE JUST HEARD, JOHN
STREBELON WOULD BE AT YOUR FEET, THE HAPPIEST OF HUSBANDS, THE
PROUDEST OF FATHERS. ONCE MORE I TELL YOU, CHILD, YOU ARE RE-
PEATING MY MISTAKE AND YOUR OWN.
:ENTER LIZETTE, UPPER DOOR.:

LIZETTE.

MRS. BROWN IS WAITING TO SEE YOU IN YOUR OWN ROOMS, MRS. HOLCOMB.

FANNY.

TELL HER I WILL BE THERE IN A MOMENT. :EXIT LIZETTE.: I WISH
SHE HAD CHOSEN SOME OTHER TIME. :RISING.: I WOULD AGAIN, I DO
AGAIN URGE FOR YOUR OWN SAKE, FOR YOUR CHILD'S SAKE, LILLIAN--
ABOVE ALL, FOR YOUR HUSBAND'S SAKE-- TO WRITE TO HIM-- UNVEIL YOUR
HEART-- LET HIM SEE HIMSELF THERE BESIDE HIS CHILD-- AND THE PAST
WILL BE ATONED FOR BY A PEACEFUL AND HAPPY FUTURE, BELIEVE ME.
:GOES TOWARD UPPER DOOR.:

MRS. BROWN.

:CALLING.: MRS. HOLCOMB!

FANNY.

I MUST GO-- I HEAR NATALIE-- :MRS. BROWN CALLING AGAIN.: COMING.
:LOUDER.: I'M COMING UP, MRS. BROWN. :EXITS R, U, D.:

LILL.

:SOLUS, RISING.: NO-- I DARE NOT WRITE TO HIM-- I DARE NOT ASK
HIM TO RETURN TO ME-- THOUGH I KNOW MY HEART WILL BREAK IF HE RE-
MAINS AWAY. :STOPS AS IF IN THOUGHT. CALLS.: NATALIE!

NATALIE.

:RUNNING IN R.: HERE I AM, MAMMA! AND HERE IS DOLLY-- WE'VE
BEEN PUTTING HER HOUSE TO RIGHTS.

10

LILL.

<u>SITTING IN CHAIR USED BY FANNY, AND PLACING NATALIE ON THE STOOL
SHE, HERSELF HAD USED.</u> TELL ME, DEAR, HOW LONG IS IT SINCE YOU
SENT THE LETTER TO PAPA.

NAT.

THE ONE YOU SPELT FOR ME?

LILL.

YES?

NAT.

<u>TIMIDLY.</u>   I-- I SENT ANOTHER SINCE.

LILL.

<u>ASTONISHED.</u>   ANOTHER?

NAT.

YES-- I ASKED UNCLE BABBAGE TO PUT THE POST OFFICE PICTURE ON FOR
ME-- AND PUT IT IN THE BOX.   WAS IT NAUGHTY?

LILL.

IT IS NEVER NAUGHTY FOR YOU TO WRITE TO DEAR PAPA.   BUT YOU SHOWED
ME ALL YOUR OTHER LETTERS.

NAT.

<u>ASSUMING IMPORTANCE.</u>   OH-- I WANTED TO SAY SOMETHING IMPORTANT
TO PAPA.

LILL.

YOU NEED NEVER SHOW ME YOUR LETTERS TO HIM UNLESS YOU PLEASE-- BUT
HOW DID YOU DIRECT IT?

NAT.

AUNTY BROWN WROTE ON THE ENVELOPE.

LILL.

WOULD YOU LIKE TO WRITE TO PAPA, TO-DAY?

NAT.

<u>CLAPPING HER HANDS.</u>   OH, YES-- YES.

11

LILL.
AND LET ME TELL YOU WHAT TO WRITE?

NAT.
:SPRINGING UP.:   OH, THAT'LL MAKE IT SO EASY.   :RUNS TO DRAWER,
GETS PAPER AND ENVELOPE, TAKES THEM TO TABLE.   LILL. PUTS HASSOCK
ON CHAIR AND LIFTS NAT. TO ENABLE HER TO SIT ON IT. NAT. TAKES
PEN.:   NOW, MAMMA, WHAT AM I TO SAY?

LILL.
DEAR PAPA.

NAT.
:WRITING.:   THAT'S EASY.   NOW?

LILL.
I DO HOPE-- ON THE LINE BELOW, DEAR.

NAT.
:WRITING.:   DO OPE.

LILL.
HOPE.   THAT'S IT.   YOU WILL COME BACK TO AMERICA.

NAT.
:SPELLING AS SHE WRITES.:   K- U- M- COME--

LILL.
OH DEAR, NO! LET ME GUIDE YOUR HAND.   :GUIDES NATALIE'S HAND,
SPEAKING THE WORDS AS SHE CAUSES THE CHILD TO TRACE THEM.:   COME,
C- O- M- E- BACK TO AMERICA, :WITH EMOTION.:   MAMA WANTS YOU VERY
MUCH.   :SOBBING.:   SO VERY MUCH.   SHE-- WILL-- DIE, IF YOU DO
NOT COME-- COME BACK TO HER, TO ME.
                      :LILL. SOBBING FALLS ON OTTOMAN.:

NAT.
WHY THAT'S JUST WHAT I WROTE IN THE LETTER I DID NOT SHOW YOU.

LILL.
:TURNING HER FACE FROM CHILD.:   WHAT YOU WROTE?

NAT.
:LOOKING AT LETTER.:   YES.   I KNEW YOU WANTED HIM TO COME BACK.

12

I TOLD HIM WHAT LIZETTE TOLD ME WHEN SHE HELPED ME TO WRITE.

LILL.
:CONTROLLING HERSELF.: WHAT DID SHE TELL YOU?

NAT.
THAT THE DOCTOR SAID YOU MIGHT GO AWAY IF HE DID NOT COME BACK
SOON-- AND THEN YOU KNOW HE COULD NOT FIND YOU AT ALL.

LILL.
:CATCHING CHILD TO HER BREAST.: OH, MY DARLING! MY DARLING!
:KISSES HER.:

NAT.
I PUT THE PICTURE OF YOU THAT YOU GAVE ME LAST CHRISTMAS INTO THE
LETTER FOR PAPA TO SEE.

LILL.
:TURNING AWAY, FROM NATALIE AS SERVANT ENTERS LOWER DOOR.: OH, JOHN.
JOHN. IF YOU BUT KNEW MY HEART TO-DAY AS WELL AS YOU KNOW MY
FACE. :SEES SERVANT.: WELL?

LIZETTE.
:WITH LETTERS ON SALVER.: THE MAIL, MADAME. TWO LETTERS FOR
MR. WESTBROOK AND ONE FOR MISS NATALIE.
:NATALIE RUNS TO LIZETTE WHO GIVES HER
LETTER AND EXITS UPPER DOOR.:

NAT.
:LOOKING AT LETTER.: OH, WHAT A DIRTY LETTER! THAT ISN'T FROM
PAPA.

LILL.
LET ME READ IT FOR YOU. :TAKES LETTER-- LOOKS AT IT.: IT IS
FROM PAPA. :STOPS.:

NAT.
WHAT MAKES IT SO UGLY?

LILL.
:LOOKING AT LETTER.: IT IS STAINED WITH SEA WATER-- STEAMSHIP
HANOVER! THE STEAMER THAT WAS WRECKED-- NATALIE, THIS LETTER WAS
AT THE BOTTOM OF THE BIG OCEAN.

13

NAT.
AND THEY GOT IT OUT AGAIN?

LILL.
YES-- AND SENT IT TO YOU.

NAT.
OH, THEY KNEW IT WAS FROM MY PAPA. DO READ IT.

LILL.
:OPENS LETTER. PICTURE FALLS OUT.: WHAT IS THAT?

NAT.
:PICKING IT UP, LOOKS AT IT.: SEE! MAMA-- PAPA'S PICTURE.

LILL.
:TAKES PICTURE, LOOKS AT IT-- IN DEEP EMOTION.: HIS HAIR IS AL-
MOST WHITE NOW-- AND IN THREE YEARS! :KISSES PICTURE.:

NAT.
WHAT'S IN THE LETTER?

LILL.
:READS.: ''MY LITTLE DARLING, I WILL TAKE THE NEXT STEAMER FOR
AMERICA!'' THE NEXT STEAMER FOR AMERICA--

NAT.
I'M SO GLAD-- SO GLAD! :CLINGS TO HER MOTHER'S DRESS.:

LILL.
:LOOKING AT DATE.: AUGUST THE ELEVENTH-- NATALIE, NATALIE-- PAPA
MAY BE IN AMERICA-- NOW--
:ENTER FLORENCE, UPPER DOOR.:

FLOR.
:STOPPING UP STAGE.: WHY, LILLIAN, WHAT'S THE MATTER?

LILL.
FLORENCE! NATALIE'S FATHER-- MY-- MR. STREBELON IS COMING HOME.

FLOR.
OH, HE'S FOUND HIS SENSES AT LAST, HAS HE?

14

LILL.

THE NEWS HAS EXCITED ME A LITTLE, AND I MUST TELL MY FATHER.

NAT.

:PULLING HER MOTHER UP STAGE.: YES-- YES, WE MUST TELL GRANDPA'
AND UNCLE BABBAGE.

LILL.

:TO FLORENCE.: YOU'LL EXCUSE ME-- A FEW MINUTES.

FLOR.

CERTAINLY.

:EXIT UPPER DOOR, LILL, AND NATALIE.:

FLOR.

:SOLUS.: NOW, I AM REALLY GLAD OF THAT-- LILL WAS BREAKING HER
HEART . . . . POOR THING, I DON'T WONDER AT IT. WHAT'S THE USE
OF A HUSBAND TWO THOUSAND MILES AWAY? :ENTER PHIPPS PRECEDED BY
LIZETTE.: PHIPPS!

PHIPPS.

BROWN!

FLOR.

RETURNED FROM EUROPE.

PHIPPS. ,

JUST OFF THE STEAMER. :TO LIZETTE.: GIVE THIS CARD AND THIS
NOTE TO MRS. HOLCOMB, AND TELL HER I AM AT HER SERVICE. :EXIT
LIZETTE.: :TO FLOR.: JUST REACHED THE DOCK. BUSINESS TOUR IN
EUROPE THIS TIME. WASTED NO TIME ON SIGHT SEEING AS I DID THREE
YEARS AGO.

FLOR.

WHAT STEAMER DID YOU COME IN?

PHIPPS.

VEAL DEE PAREE. LESS THAN HALF AN HOUR AGO! STREBELON AND I
JUMPED INTO A CARRIAGE AS SOON AS WE TOUCHED THE PIER.

FLOR.

JOHN STREBELON!

15

PHIPPS.

LEFT BAGGAGE TO THE CURIOSITY OF THE OFFICIALS OF THE CUSTOM HOUSE.
ONLY A SMALL VALISE-- BOX OR TWO OF COLLARS, A FEW NECKTIES-- HALF
A DOZEN SHIRTS . . . .

FLOR.

MR. PHIPPS, PLEASE GIVE MY IMAGINATION SOME CHANCE. BUT MR.
STREBELON?

PHIPPS.

IS AT HIS HOTEL. HE WAS IN SUCH A HURRY TO SEE HIS CHILD, HE
COULD SCARCE WAIT FOR THE VEAL DEE PAREE TO SWING TO. THE NOTE
I BROUGHT WAS FROM HIM-- HE WANTS ME TO TAKE NATALIE TO HIM IN THE
CARRIAGE I HAVE BELOW-- HE'S CRAZY TO SEE THE CHILD.

FLOR.

INDEED! AND LILLIAN-- HIS WIFE? HAS HE FORGOTTEN HER?

PHIPPS.

THINKS AND TALKS TO ME OF NOTHING ELSE-- DID ALL THE VOYAGE-- I
TRIED HIM ON DRY GOODS. NO USE! HE TOOK NO MORE INTEREST IN THE
NEW STYLES OF IMPORTED BROCADES-- THAT REMINDS ME! :TAKES OUT
WATCH-- THEN NOTE BOOK.: I MUST NOT FORGET TO-- :TO FLOR.: EX-
CUSE ME, BUT I MUST GET TO THE BANK BEFORE THREE O'CLOCK. LET ME
SEE, :READING NOTES.: ARNOLD MATTHESON & CO.-- AXMINSTER CAR-
PETS-- FIVE AND TEN OFF . . . .
:ENTER FANNY, UPPER DOOR.:

FANNY.

MR; PHIPPS.

PHIPPS.

AH! GLAD TO SEE YOU-- JUST BACK FROM EUROPE-- GET STREBELON'S
NOTE?

FANNY.

I HAVE ASKED MR. STREBELON TO CALL HERE AND SEE HER.

PHIPPS.

:NODS.: RIGHT. I UNDERSTAND-- AND MRS. STREBELON . . .

FANNY.

I AM NOW GOING TO TELL HER. YOU WILL EXCUSE ME?

                    PHIPPS.
CERTAINLY.   :EXIT FANNY.:   MRS. HOLCOMB HAS WHAT I CALL HORSE
SENSE-- MOST WOMEN HAVE.

                    FLOR.
YOU THINK SO?

                    PHIPPS.
:RETURNING TO HIS NOTES.:   YES-- OLD WOMEN.

                    FLOR.
OH!

                    PHIPPS.
:AT HIS NOTES.:   LONG ISLAND MANUFACTURING COMPANY, I WONDER IF
I CAN RUN OVER TO GREENPOINT!   IT WILL DO TO-MORROW-- BY THE WAY--
MRS. BROWN-- WHILE I THINK OF IT-- MERRILL, COOK & CO., HALF PAST--
DRAFT ON LONDON-- MUST NOT FORGET THAT.   :TO FLOR.:   YOU HAVE
NOW BEEN A WIDOW UPWARDS OF TWO YEARS, I BELIEVE.

                    FLOR.
TWO YEARS, TO-MORROW.

                    PHIPPS.
:AT HIS NOTES.:   WHITBECK, OLDHANGER & CO., ORDER FILLED PER SAM-
PLE-- :LOOKS AT HIS WATCH.:   HALF PAST TWO. :TO FLOR.:   WILL YOU
BE MY WIFE, MRS. BROWN? :LOOKING AT HER AS HE CLOSES HIS WATCH.
                    PUTS IT INTO HIS POCKET AND THEN RETURNS
                    TO HIS NOTES.:

                    FLOR.
SIR!

                    PHIPPS.
WILL- YOU- BE- MY- WIFE? :AT NOTE AGAIN.:   SORRY I COULD NOT GET
THOSE GOODS FOR JONES & CUNNINGHAM.   :TO FLOR.:   I WILL DROP IN
AND SEE YOU THIS AFTERNOON.
                    :FLORENCE STAGGERS-- HE CATCHES HER IN HIS
                    ARM.   PLACES ON OTTOMAN.   PAUSE.   SHE
                    JUMPS UP QUICKLY.:

                    FLOR.

EVER STRUCK BY A CANNON BALL?

                    PHIPPS,
NO.   I WAS HIT BY A BASE BALL, ONCE.

                    FLOR,
THEN YOU CANNOT APPRECIATE MY FEELINGS AT THE PRESENT MOMENT.
:SURVEYS HIM.:   I RATHER LIKE YOU, PHIPPS-- YOU'RE NOT HANDSOME--
BUT YOU INTEREST ME.   THE DOCTOR HAS PRESCRIBED A SECOND HUSBAND.

                    PHIPPS,
OF COURSE.   THAT IS THE ONLY PRESCRIPTION THAT CAN CURE A WIDOW
OF HER WIDOWHOOD.

                    FLOR.
I MIGHT AS WELL TAKE THE DOSE IN ONE FORM AS ANOTHER.   I WILL
SWALLOW IT WITH MY EYES SHUT.

                    PHIPPS,
I'M NOT A SUGAR-COATED PILL, MADAME-- BUT--

                    FLOR.
:LAUGHS.:   PHIPPS, THERE'S MY HAND.

                    PHIPPS,
:KISSES HER HAND. RETURNS TO HIS NOTES.:   SEPTEMBER SECOND--
SUPPOSE WE CALL IT THIRTY DAYS AFTER DATE?   :WRITES.:

                    FLOR.
THIRTY DAYS FROM DATE.

                    PHIPPS,
YES-- BY THE WAY, WHAT IS YOUR MIDDLE NAME?

                    FLOR.
FLORENCE ST. VINCENT BROWN.   HAVE YOU A CARD ABOUT YOU?   :HE
GIVES HER CARD.:   THANK YOU.   :READS CARD.:   GEORGE WASHINGTON
PHIPPS.   I SHOULDN'T LIKE TO FORGET YOUR NAME BEFORE THE HAPPY
DAY.   :CROSSING TO R.:

                    PHIPPS,
EASILY REMEMBERED.   FATHER OF HIS COUNTRY PHIPPS.

18

FLOR.
NOW DON'T FORGET, PHIPPS, OCTOBER SECOND.

PHIPPS.
OCTOBER FIFTH.

FLOR.
EH?

PHIPPS.
THREE DAYS GRACE, YOU KNOW. :FLOR. LAUGHS. PHIPPS WRITING IN
NOTE BOOK.: OCTOBER 2ND AND 5TH. WE SHALL BOTH FALL DUE ON THE
SAME DAY. SAY HALF PAST THREE P. M.

FLOR.
HALF PAST THREE P. M.

PHIPPS.
SHARP!

FLOR.
SHARP! :LAUGHS. EXITS UPPER DOOR R.:

PHIPPS.
:SOLUS. LOOKS AT HIS WATCH-- AFTER FLORENCE.: HM! I CAN GIVE
HER SEVENTEEN MINUTES MORE.: :EXITS AFTER FLOR.:
                                :STAGE REMAINS EMPTY A FEW MINUTES.
                                ENTER LIZETTE AND STREBELON, R. H. LOWER
                                DOOR.:

STREB.
I WILL WAIT. :SOLUS. LOOKING ROUND HIM.: THE VERY ROOM! HERE,
ON THIS VERY SPOT IT WAS, SHE GAVE ME HER HAND. AS I STAND HERE,
IT SEEMS BUT YESTERDAY-- YESTERDAY IT SEEMED AN AGE!

FANNY.
:ENTERS UPPER DOOR.: MR. STREBELON!

STREBELON.
:TURNING TO HER. MRS. HOLCOMB!
                                :THEY GO TO EACH OTHER AND SHAKE HANDS.:

19

FANNY.

I AM VERY, VERY GLAD TO SEE YOU HERE-- HERE IN THIS HOUSE, ONCE MORE, MR. STREBELON.

STREB.

I KNOW YOU ARE-- I UNDERSTAND AND THANK YOU.

FANNY.

MR. PHIPPS BROUGHT ME YOUR REQUEST TO SEND NATALIE TO YOU. IN JUSTICE TO LILLIAN I COULD NOT DO THAT. I FELT AS YOU MUST FEEL, THAT THE PROPER PLACE FOR YOU TO SEE YOUR CHILD WAS WHERE HER MOTHER IS.

STREB.

TELL ME OF HER. HOW IS LILLIAN?

FANNY.

AS WELL AS SHE HAS BEEN ANY DAY SINCE SHE RETURNED HERE. THE NEWS OF YOUR ARRIVAL HAS EXCITED HER A LITTLE-- BUT YOU SHALL SEE HER FOR YOURSELF.

STREB.

SEE HER-- SEE HER?

FANNY,

I WILL SEND HER TO YOU.

NAT.

:RUNNING IN.: OH, AUNT FANNY, WHEN WILL PAPA BE HERE--
:SEES STREBELON. CATCHES HOLD OF AUNT
FANNY'S DRESS, AND HIDES BEHIND IT, PEEP-
ING OUT AT STREBELON.:

STREB.

:HOLDING HIS ARMS OUT TO HER.: NATALIE, DON'T YOU KNOW ME?

NAT.

:COMES FORWARD A LITTLE-- LOOKS AT STREBELON. UTTERS A CRY AND
RUSHES TO HIM.: OH, PAPA! PAPA!

STREB.

:TAKING HER IN HIS ARMS.: NATALIE-- MY CHILD! MY OWN DARLING--

20

:AUNT FANNY STEALS SILENTLY TO DOOR.:

STREB,
:SITTING AND HOLDING THE CHILD OUT IN FRONT OF HIM.:   AND YOU DID
NOT KNOW ME?

NAT,
O, YES, I DID-- BUT YOUR HAIR IS SO WHITE-- JUST LIKE YOUR PICTURE.
OH, I'M SO GLAD-- AND--

STREB,
:KISSING HER, THEN LOOKING AT HER.:   HOW YOU HAVE GROWN-- AND YOUR
HAIR IS DARKER-- HOW LIKE HER MOTHER. :KISSES HER AGAIN.

:AUNT FANNY STEALS OUT UPPER DOOR.:

NAT,
IT WAS NAUGHTY IN YOU TO STAY AWAY SO LONG. I KNEW YOU'D COME
WHEN I WROTE YOU HOW MUCH MAMA WANTED TO HAVE YOU HERE-- AND HOW
UNHAPPY SHE WAS WITHOUT YOU.   BUT WHAT ARE YOU THINKING ABOUT?

STREB,
I CAME AS SOON AS I RECEIVED YOUR LAST LETTER--

NAT,
I KNEW YOU WOULD.

STREBELON,
:THOUGHTFULLY.:   YOU WROTE ME A GREAT MANY LETTERS.

NAT,
:PROUDLY.:   DIDN'T I?   IT WAS HARD AT FIRST; BUT MAMA TOLD ME
WHAT TO WRITE, YOU KNOW.

STREB.
:EAGERLY.:   YES-- YES.   MAMMA TOLD YOU WHAT TO SAY TO PAPA.
AND-- AND-- AND, IN THE LAST LETTERS, SHE TOLD YOU TO SAY HOW UN-
HAPPY MAMMA WAS WITHOUT PAPA!   THE WORDS CAME FROM HER--

NAT,

MAMMA DID NOT KNOW ANYTHING ABOUT THE LAST LETTER-- AUNTY BROWN

HELPED ME TO WRITE THAT-- AND UNCLE BABBAGE PUT IT IN THE BOX FOR
ROME.

                          STREB.
:RISING AND TURNING AWAY FROM NATALIE.:   AND . . .   AND YOUR MAMMA
KNEW NOTHING ABOUT WHAT WAS IT IN.

                          NAT.
:PROUDLY.   NOT A WORD.   I DID IT MYSELF.   :GOES UP FOR DOLL.:

                          STREB.
:TO HIMSELF.:   AND I THOUGHT HER HAND HAD GUIDED HERS,   AND THAT
SHE CALLED THE HUSBAND WHILE THE CHILD CALLED HER FATHER!   :PAUSE:
''MAMMA IS VERY UNHAPPY WITHOUT YOU.''   IT WAS NOT SHE WHO SAID
IT-- NOT SHE-- HER HEART IS SILENT STILL!   :RINGS BELL. RISES.:

                          NAT.
:COMING DOWN TO HIM.:   WHAT'S THE MATTER, PAPA?   YOU'RE-NOT GOING
TO CRY-- MAMMA CRIES-- BUT PAPAS NEVER DO-- DO THEY?

                          STREB.
THEY OFTEN HAVE MOST CAUSE!   :CROSSES TO C.   ENTER LIZETTE.:
YOU MAY SAY TO MRS. STREBELON THAT I CANNOT WAIT AT PRESENT-- I
HAVE AN ENGAGEMENT-- I MAY CALL-- I MEAN I WILL RETURN . . .
:EXIT LIZETTE, LOWER DOOR.:   GOOD BYE, NATALIE--   :TAKING CHILD
IN HIS ARMS.:   GOOD BYE.--   :KISSES HER.:

                          NAT.
GOOD BYE?

                          STREB.
YES-- PAPA MUST GO NOW.

                          NAT.
WHY, PAPA, YOU'VE NOT SEEN MAMMA, YET!

                          STREB.
I KNOW, DEAR-- I KNOW-- BUT I MUST GO NOW-- I MUST.
                    :PLACES CHILD ON GROUND. GOES TOWARD
                    LOWER DOOR AS LILLIAN ENTERS UPPER DOOR.:

                          LILL.

STREB.

[TURNS QUICKLY.] LILLIAN! [PAUSE. CHILD LOOKING AT BOTH
IN WONDER.] LILLIAN, I AM GLAD TO SEE YOU--
[GOES TO MEET HER, EXTENDS HIS HANDS TO
HER FRANKLY. SHE TAKES IT TIMIDLY.]

LILL.

YOU WERE GOING-- WITHOUT-- WITHOUT SEEING ME!

STREB.

[EMBARRASSED.] BELIEVE, ME, I AM-- AM GLAD, MORE THAN GLAD TO SEE
YOU. BUT I FELT I HAD NO RIGHT TO BRING ABOUT SUCH A MEETING
WITHOUT YOUR OWN EXPRESS DESIRE. WHEN LAST WE PARTED I PLEDGED
MYSELF TO THAT. I UNDERSTAND YOUR LONG-- LONG SILENCE PERFECTLY.

LILL.

PART AGAIN! [ASIDE, CROSSING TO L. H.] I KNEW IT!

NAT.

[WHO BY HER MOTHER'S SIDE HAS BEEN WONDERINGLY LISTENING.] OH,
PAPA-- DON'T GO AWAY.

STREB.

[TAKING HER UP.] PAPA MUST GO-- GOOD BYE, LILLIAN.
[HOLDS OUT HIS HAND TO LILL. AS LIL-
LIAN STEPS TO TAKE IT, HER HEAD AVERTED,
NATALIE WHO HAS ONE ARM ROUND STREB.'S
NECK PUTS THE OTHER ROUND LILL. TRYING TO
DRAW THEM TOGETHER.]

NAT.

KISS MAMMA.

[LILL AND STREBELON'S EYES MEET. HERS
ARE FULL OF TEARS. THEY AVERT THEIR
HEADS FROM EACH OTHER. NAT LOOKS FROM
ONE TO THE OTHER. PAUSE.]

STREB.

[MASTERING HIS EMOTION, PUTTING DOWN NATALIE.] THERE, THERE,
NATALIE-- GOOD BYE-- FAREWELL, LILLIAN, FOREVER.

                                LILL.
FOREVER!

                                STREB.
FOR THREE YEARS YOUR HEART HAS BEEN SILENT-- WILL IT SPEAK LATER,
THINK YOU?
                        :LILLIAN IS SOBBING.:

                                NAT.
OH, PAPA-- I FORGOT-- MY LAST LETTER. :RUNS TO TABLE. TAKES LET-
TER.: HERE IT IS. :CROSSES TO C.: MAMMA AND I WROTE IT THIS
MORNING-- SHE HELD MY HAND. :GIVES HIM LETTER.:

                                STREB.
:TAKING LETTER, ABOUT TO PUT IT IN HIS POCKET.: I'LL ANSWER IT
SOON, DEAR.

                                NAT.
OH, READ IT NOW-- PAPA.

                                STREB.
:READING.: DEAR PAPA . . . . MAMMA WANTS YOU VERY MUCH.
                        :READS LETTER. STOPS, LOOKS AT LILLIAN.:

                                LILL.
JOHN!

                                STREB.
LILLIAN, LILLIAN! CAN YOU REPEAT THESE WORDS WITH YOUR OWN LIPS?

                                LILL.
WITH MY WHOLE HEART-- JOHN. WITH MY HEART THAT KNOWS NOW HOW
MUCH IT LOVES YOU. :THROWS HERSELF INTO HIS ARMS-- AS FANNY
                        ENTERS STEADILY UPPER DOOR.:

                                STREB.
:EMBRACING HER.: MY OWN WIFE-- MY WIFE!
                        :ENTER UPPER DOOR, WESTBROOK AND BABBAGE,
                        FOLLOWING FANNY, AND PHIPPS, AT LOWER DOOR
                        FOLLOWING FLORENCE.:

FANNY,
:DEMURELY,: I BEG YOUR PARDON, I WAS LOOKING FOR MRS. BROWN,

FLORENCE,
:SAME AIR,: I BEG YOUR PARDON, I WAS LOOKING FOR MRS. HOLCOMB,

PHIPPS,
AH, STREBELON-- LET ME PRESENT MY FUTURE WIFE-- MRS. GEO. WASHING-
TON, EASILY REMEMBERED, THE MOTHER OF HER COUNTRY-- PHIPPS!

:LILL, RUNS TO TABLE-- SITS DOWN, NATALIE
BESIDE HER,:

WEST,
:TO BABBAGE,: MY CONSCIENCE IS AT REST AT LAST!

BABBAGE,
MINE IS MORE EASY,

STREB,
:GOES TO HIS WIFE, TURNS ROUND, HOLDS OUT HIS HAND TO WEST,:
IN THE FUTURE BEFORE US, LET US FORGIVE AND FORGET THE PAST,

BABB,
AND RETIRING FROM BUSINESS, SPECULATE NO MORE IN HUMAN HEARTS,

C U R T A I N,

---0-0-0---